This story is dedicated
to the loving memory
of my sister,

Bonnie Jean Foster,

who always went first
to show me the way.

First Montag Press E-Book and Paperback Original Edition September 2013

Montag Press
ISBN: 978-1-940233-01-7
Cover art © 2013 Jason Mowry
Cover design © 2013 Rick Febré
Author photo © 2013 Patricia A. Bussard

Montag Press Team:
Project Editor – Mara Hodges
Layout & E-Book Designer – Rick Febré
Managing Director – Charlie Franco

A Montag Press Book
www.montagpress.com
Montag Press
536 E. 8th Street
Davis CA, 95616 USA

Montag Press, the burning book with the hatchet cover, the skewed word mark and the portrayal of the long-suffering fireman mascot are trademarks of Montag Press.

Printed & Digitally Originated in the United States of America
10 9 8 7 6 5 4 3 2 1

STINGER STARS

BY PAUL A. BUSSARD

ACKNOWLEDGEMENTS

THANKS to my sister Bonnie for the many enjoyable hours we spent playing with plot ideas in the early stages of writing this story.

THANKS to the Northpoint writers, H.W. "Buzz" Bernard, Dr. Terry Segal, Terri DelCampo, and Mark All for their ideas, encouragement, and critiques of the fledgling manuscript.

THANKS to the members of Writers In The Hat for their in-depth evaluation of the developing story. "Show, don't tell." (grin)

THANKS to the members of The Woodlands Writers' Guild for their constructive criticisms and encouraging support.

VERY SPECIAL THANKS to Kathryn Wilham, managing editor of Aqueduct Press, who could have sent me a form rejection letter, but instead sent me three pages of constructive feedback that very likely made the difference between getting published, or not. Thank you, Kath, for your altruistic dedication to improving the craft of writing.

THANKS to my editor, (Happy) Mara Hodges, whose every suggestion made the story better.

Finally, THANKS to my illustrator, Jason Mowry, for a fantastic cover.

As Oprah says—"It takes a village." THANKS to my village.

Paul A. Bussard

STINGER STARS

by Paul A. Bussard

-ſ-

Information — the coding of perceptions into patterns.
Knowledge — the realization of *information* in the mind.
Intelligence — the ability to reason about *knowledge.*
Sapience — the wisdom to manifest *intelligence*—or not.

—P.A.B.

CRITTER

EL PASO, TEXAS:

Maria de la Cruz parked her hand-me-down Corolla in the west lot of the Martinson Genetics research facility. She wrinkled her nose at the chemical stench coming from the *maquila* plastics factory across the Rio Grande. The construction on I-10 had delayed her so much, she'd been late to class, now late to work. She even missed getting her habitual Venti green tea at Starbucks.

The five-story M-Gen building shimmered in the late afternoon heat waves rising from the broiling parking lot. Blinding sunlight reflected from the west wall of windows, forcing her to shield her eyes.

She hurried toward the rear entrance, swiped her badge, and opened the door to the aquatics lab, savoring the cool rush of air that unfurled her long black hair and pinned her cotton print dress against her trim figure. With the breeze came the familiar waterfront smell. No amount of air conditioning or filtration could remove the odor of several dozen aquariums and terrariums that filled the room. By the time she closed her locker and donned her lab coat, she'd already become accustomed to the smell.

She surveyed her domain—a long, rectangular room with stark white ceramic tile walls that reminded her of a large public restroom. The impression was intensified by the occasional gurgling sounds emanating from the exposed plumbing overhead that served the genetics clean room on the floor above. Next year she'd be up there, working on her doctorate. Maybe. If she didn't hurry up and finish her thesis, she might not even get her Master's.

Maria counted her blessings. Working four to midnight allowed her to hide her stunted arm from the stares of coworkers. It also enabled her to attend classes at the University of Texas in El Paso during the day. One of her professors at UTEP had helped her get the job at M-Gen.

She started her rounds, humming while she dropped prescribed amounts of specialized foods into each tank according to species and making entries in the logbooks—difficult while wearing the protocol-required elbow-length gloves.

A young man with kinky red hair and freckled face appeared at the double doors connecting to the office wing. All thoughts of thesis research disappeared from Maria's mind.

"Alex—," she interrupted herself and smiled, "I mean *Doctor* Goodson. Aren't you afraid you'll hurt your new image, coming to the aquatics lab?"

"Don't start with the 'Doctor' stuff," he said, walking down the row of tanks to join her. "Oh, I'm proud to finally have my Ph.D., but I'm still the same guy I was when I had your job, and still at the bottom of the food chain here."

"No." Maria shook her head. "I hold that position."

"Not in my book."

She smiled. Alex had always treated her as an equal and a friend—never talking down to her. He was apparently even comfortable with her arm, unlike the rest of the staff. She wished their shifts overlapped more so she could spend more time with him.

"Thanks, Alex. Most people who work here don't even know I'm a student. They think I'm part of the janitorial staff—the girl who cleans the aquariums at night." She looked at the tanks, then at Alex, giving him a disgusted look. "Okay, I do clean the tanks, but I also study the animals that are in them. I wonder how many of the research staff know that skinks eat spinach or that octopuses grit their teeth."

"I didn't even know they had teeth."

She smiled at his admission and continued making her rounds. Alex walked with her.

"They don't, really. They have a rasp-like tongue—a radula. It nearly drove me crazy hunting down the source of the sound. It's creepy enough working the late shift alone without hearing things that go 'grit' in the night."

Alex laughed, and Maria couldn't help joining him.

She remembered that night vividly—going from one tank to another until she located the one the sound was coming from. She just happened to be looking when the octopus spit out a mouthful of crab shell from which it had been scraping flesh.

When Maria came to the next tank, her hand suddenly flew to her mouth and she screamed. "Alex, *Dios mío!*"

Alex rushed to her side. "What is it, Maria? What's wrong?"

"The starfish! Someone has cut off their arms!" She stared at him, aghast. "Who would do such a horrible thing?"

Inside the aquarium, more than a dozen New Zeland starfish, *Coscinasterias calamaria*, attempted to crawl across the gravel bottom and each other—clumsily—one or more missing arms hampering their progress. Stumps of anemic raw flesh showed where their appendages had been severed.

Alex peered into the tank, then nodded. "It had to be Doug," he said. His lips pressed tightly together. "He asked me to check on 'em while he's in Peru."

"You knew?" She glared at him as if he were responsible, disappointed to learn he might not have come just to see her.

"I knew about the experiment. But I didn't know he'd carried it to such extremes."

"Alex, we have to tell Dr. Martinson."

The idea that Doug—*anyone*—could commit such an atrocity disturbed her deeply. She couldn't allow it to go unreported. Alex shook his head. He told her several of the staff had already complained about that kind of regeneration research to no avail.

"This is not research. It's animal cruelty! Look at that," she yelled, pointing to the aquarium. "He's cut every starfish in the tank!" She cradled her stunted arm protectively.

"Maria, I guess I understand why you'd be upset about him cuttin' off their arms, I mean … uh … ," he glanced meaningfully at her arm, "… but you must have known things like this happened at M-Gen."

She knew that animals would be used in experiments—she would even perform some of them herself. "But I never expected anything as inhumane as this." She waved her good arm at the starfish tank. She tried to calm down. It wasn't Alex's fault. Yelling at him wouldn't accomplish anything, but it was hard for her to keep her emotions in check.

"M-Gen is a genetics research company. We're supposed to be looking for gene sequences controlling regeneration, not mutilating defenseless animals." She managed to get her voice back down to its normal range.

"Yeah, well, Doug didn't make it as a geneticist. He couldn't DNA sequence his way out of a paper bag."

"Then why does he have to do *anything*?" she asked, angry again.

"He's a manager. You haven't been here long enough to know, but Dr. M. requires managers to do a minimum amount of lab work each quarter. Including his son. He says it helps the managers keep their ideas grounded in reality. So, this is what Doug does. He'll prob'ly create a multi-layered chart showin' growth rates versus number of arms chopped off just so he has something to show on his quarterly progress report."

"You mean he does this regularly?" Maria's voice rose to a squeak.

"Often enough. He's cut off lizard legs and salamander tails before … chopped up flatworms, of course, now starfish arms. Any animal unlucky enough to have some sort of appendage is fair game to him."

Maria pictured Doug as a child gleefully plucking wings

off of butterflies just to watch them crawl around helplessly. She clenched her hands into fists. "He's got to be stopped. When I interviewed for this job I told Dr. Martinson that I wanted to help people recover lost limbs—to enable them to be whole again. Now I find that his son practices *dismemberment!*"

"What are you gonna do?"

"I'm going to demand that Dr. Martinson put an end to this inhumane practice. It's against company ethics. I know, because I reviewed them before I agreed to work here."

Alex raised an eyebrow. "That could have some serious consequences."

"What? You think Dr. Martinson would fire me? Did he fire any of the others who protested? No." She answered the question herself. "Of course they were *men* with Ph.D.'s." Her words dripped with scorn. It suddenly occurred to her that Alex now fell into that category, but she didn't amend her criticism. Her thesis advisor had warned her about the Good Ol' Boy system when he suggested she work for M-Gen.

"Well, yeah," he admitted, "but even if he doesn't fire you, Doug'll sure make your life miserable if he finds out you were the one who complained."

"Miserable?" she shrilled. "What do you think he's made these starfish? At least I have a voice with which to defend myself. Just because I'm not a member of PETA doesn't mean I can't speak up for them. These poor animals … ." She turned to point at the tank, but stopped mid-sentence. "Oh, *por el amor de Dios!* Alex, he only left one arm on that one. I can't stand it. Please put it out of its misery." She couldn't get out of the room fast enough.

"*Qué atrocidad! Qué situación tan intolerable!*"

Alex watched her leave, then turned to open the aquarium.

* * *

TWO DAYS LATER:

Maria managed to quell her anger after the starfish incident. Alex convinced her of the futility of trying to bring Doug to justice. She immersed herself in work. She had been assigned the task of classifying all the flatworm specimens Doug had collected and sent back from Peru. The task was challenging and interesting—there were tens of thousands of species in the *platyhelminthes* phylum. Fortunately, only a fraction of that number were found in the Peruvian headwaters of the Amazon. Alex stopped by to chat with her during their shift overlap.

"Alex, I'm glad you're here," she said as he pushed through the double doors to the offices. "I wanted to talk to you about one of the flatworm specimens Doug sent back from Peru. It's acting strangely."

She waited for him to join her in front of the aquarium, one of a dozen atop a long row of tables. The tank contained a small amount of water, mucky soil, and decaying leaves. She pointed to a worm half buried in the detritus Doug had collected along with the animal. "See that one? Its color is washed out compared to the other specimens, and it's got a cut in its midsection."

Alex knelt on the stained vinyl floor. *He smells nice. Aftershave? Shampoo?*

"Yeah, I see what you mean," he said. "That might not be a cut, though. Remember flatworms sometimes reproduce asexually simply by splitting in two."

Alex lifted the tank's lid, releasing a swirl of warm, humid air, rich with the earthy smell of algae. He pulled vegetation away from the flatworm with a pair of tongs. "Well, there's the problem. It looks like it has a big Mexican sandbur—some kinda thorn—stuck in the anterior end."

Maria squatted down to peer into the tank, curious to see what he had found. The flatworm had a small, dark pronged object sticking out of it. She examined the object closely and suddenly caught her breath. "Alex, it's moving!"

"Well, sure. It's not dead, yet."

"No, not the flatworm—the *thorn*. It's pulsing and there are wiggly things where the other prongs should be."

"Wiggly things," Alex muttered.

His shoulder touched hers when he knelt beside her. She savored the intimacy for a moment, almost forgetting about the flatworm. Reluctantly, she moved aside to give him room.

"What do you think it is?" she asked.

"I dunno. It's a strange lookin' critter, that's for sure. I've never seen anything like it. The flatworm's not moving. Maybe it's been paralyzed. We need to be careful with this little guy. He could be dangerous." He moved around the tank to get a better view.

"Alex, what if it's something new? What am I supposed to do?" The prospect filled her with excitement and twinge of panic. She'd never considered the possibility that she might discover something new in her mundane job at M-Gen.

"Take notes," he advised. "If this turns out to be a new species, they'll be important in crediting you with the discovery."

"Me? You saw it before I did."

"Yeah, but you were first to recognize it was alive. Let's see if it's a known species first. Maybe nobody gets credit. Y' got a magnifyin' glass?"

Maria rose and hurried to the supply cabinets, excitement growing with each step. She grabbed a large hand-held lens and rushed back to the tank.

"I want you to examine it in detail," he said. "Tell me how you're gonna describe it in your notes. You'll hafta do better'n 'wiggly things.'"

"All right, Doctor Smartypants." She punched him on the shoulder. "I was talking to you, not defending a dissertation." His teasing criticism relaxed her.

She knelt on the hem of her lab coat and studied the strange organism for a few moments. "Okay … um … the specimen is tetrahedral with each triangular face approximately eight millimeters on a side. It has flexible appendages approximately one centimeter in length extending from each vertex. The appendages have a rounded triangular cross section tapering from about four millimeters thick at the base to two at the tip."

She looked at Alex for approval, then continued. "The specimen is covered with a smooth-textured skin, mottled gray-brown except for the tip of the appendages, around which are located three equally-spaced, colorless hemispheres, and which terminate in an ivory-colored triangular point."

"Wow, Maria. That's better'n I could've done. Lemme see the glass a minute. I want to look at those appendages."

"Oh, Alex," Maria wailed, "why does it have to have appendages? Now Doug will want to mutilate *this* animal."

"He can't. Not if there's only one specimen." He braced the lens against the window. "Look, Maria. I think that tip is some sort of beak. With the glass you can tell—it's eatin' the flatworm with it."

"Let me see," she said, suspicious that he was just trying to change the subject.

Alex handed her the magnifying glass.

She sucked in a breath. "*Santos!* Alex, did you see that? The appendage followed the motion of the lens. Those hemispheres are *eyes*. It's watching us!"

PUCALLPA

BACKWATERS OF RÍO UCAYALI, PERU:
Why in hell did I let my old man talk me into becoming a biologist?
Doug Martinson cursed himself for the hundredth time since the start of the expedition. Next he cursed his father, and then the half-naked Indians who splashed nonchalantly through the leech-infested swamp.

He flailed at an insect that buzzed too close to his ear. He missed, but it didn't matter. He had the finest mosquito net available draped over his pith helmet and tucked into his shirt collar. Nothing could get through.

Except the heat.

Sweat trickled down his neck, around his ears, and ran in rivulets down his forehead. It pooled in his eyebrows, stung his eyes and dripped from his moustache. He puffed air between compressed lips to blow the sweat out of his mouth. Mistake. Now the sweat clung to the inside of the net, obstructing his vision. "Augh!" He shook his head to try to clear the net.

The natives didn't laugh, but Doug knew he looked ridiculous in his designer safari outfit, every inch of his skin covered with some kind of protection—net, clothes, sun block, repellant, gloves. The Indians trudged along, unperturbed and unprotected, wearing shorts and little else.

Doug's hip boots were heavy, stiff, and hot. They were supposed to keep his legs and feet dry. Instead, he waded in an inch-deep puddle of his own sweat. Something—God only knew what—had worked its way into one of his boot legs. It was biting, stinging, sucking … injecting him with some exotic tropical disease from which he'd probably suffer the rest of his life.

I get stuck in this hellhole looking for friggin' flatworms, while that bastard Hendrix gets to collect starfish on some balmy beach in Hawaii.

Doug imagined himself on a tropical isle, surrounded by bare-breasted *wahines*, who competed to please their blue-eyed, blond god. They rubbed him with lotion, brought him drinks in coconuts, and fanned him with palm fronds.

"Ow! Dammit."

The palm frond became an overhanging limb he had failed to duck. The tropical island and beautiful women disappeared, replaced by the suffocating jungle and Indian porters.

The shock was almost too much for Doug. He would have abandoned this expedition long ago, but it would have put his cushy six-figure salary in jeopardy.

A half-submerged tree trunk caught his eye. "*Allí*," he shouted.

He had learned two words in Spanish for this expedition—*allí*, there, and *aquí*, here. "*Allí*. Go there. Roll over that log. *Aquí*. Come here. Turn over this rock." Ironically, the words meant nothing to the natives, who spoke only the local Indian dialect.

He took a plastic container from a porter and scooped up an inch-thick layer of rotting vegetation along with what looked like an earthworm someone had stepped on. *Platyhelminthes*. That was all he had to verify. Someone—not him—would have to figure out the rest of the classification. Of course, they'd get to do it in the comfort of an air-conditioned lab.

One more collection container left.

"*Aquí*," he yelled. He scooped under a flatworm that slowly wormed into a mucky mass of vegetation. He didn't care if he got it or not. *I'm getting out of here. Now!*

* * *

PUCALLPA, PERU:

Doug sat in an open-air bar, drinking alone and feeling sorry for himself. His plane back to the U.S. wouldn't leave until late next morning. *I'm stuck in this hole with nothing to do but listen to this infernal racket.* At that moment, a loud screech emanated from the neighboring trees. Insect? Bird? Animal? He couldn't tell, but it reminded him of his ordeal in the jungle and made him shudder. He longed for civilization and comfort and *fun.*

"Hi, there. You look as bored as I feel."

The voice startled him out of his funk. He hadn't expected anyone to speak to him in English, least of all a good-looking woman. He gave her the once-over.

A quiet whistle escaped his lips. "I'm not bored now!"

The slender woman smiled with green eyes as she set her drink on the table and slid into the chair beside him. She gave her head a quick flip. Her shoulder-length auburn hair settled obediently around her shoulders. She wore very little makeup and didn't need to.

"The bartender said another American was here. I had to see. You can't believe how sick I am of this place and how desperate I am to talk to someone in English. I'm Janie McLeod."

"Doug Martinson," he said, taking the well-manicured hand she proffered. It felt soft and cool.

Janie cocked her head and raised an eyebrow.

Whoa, she's checking me out! Doug chuckled to himself. *Fair enough, I'm checking her out, too.*

"What's a guy like you doing in a place like this?" she asked, then smiled a crooked smile as if to apologize for the worn-out cliché.

"Collecting flatworms."

"Eww." She made a face and pulled her drink closer.

Doug mentally kicked himself. *She's hot and coming on to you, and you're talking about flatworms. Nitwit.*

"Yeah, I know," he said, "but somebody's got to do it. I'm a biologist." He pulled out his wallet and handed her his business card.

"M-Gen." She nodded. Her eyes flicked from the card to his face.

He held her gaze, which seemed to take on a daring, mischievous quality. He wondered if it was his imagination or wishful thinking, but that look wasn't there earlier. "What about you?" he asked.

"Hold on. I've got a card here someplace."

Janie bent over to dig in her purse. Her loose blouse opened to give Doug a nice view of its contents. Her breasts were not big, but they were bare—all it took for him to think about getting lucky.

Well, she said she was bored. I know a thing or two we could do to change that. He forced himself to concentrate on her card. "What's a public relations rep for a Texas logging company doing in a Peruvian jungle?"

"Public relations. What else? Some of our loggers got crossways with the Indians and things got out of hand. I've been here for ten days straight," she said. "What do you do at M-Gen?"

"Regeneration research. That's the reason for the flatworms."

"What do they have to do with it?"

Several kinds of animals—flatworms, starfish, octopuses, and most amphibians—had the ability to regenerate lost or damaged body parts. Doug explained that M-Gen was looking for ways to enable human beings to do the same thing.

"Interesting," Janie replied. "I thought those kinds of companies were into genetic manipulation and creating supermen, you know—hush-hush stuff like that."

"Some might be, but I think it's mostly media hype. Dad would shit a brick—excuse the expression—if he caught anyone doing that at M-Gen. He's strictly against enhancing human genetics. His policy is to fix things that go wrong. The three R's, he calls it—restore, repair and regenerate."

"So, can you—restore, repair and regenerate?"

She appeared interested, and Doug wanted to keep her that way, but her question seemed a little too pointed. Horny or not, even he knew better than to discuss research results with a stranger.

"Well, you were right about the hush-hush part. Biotherapeutics is a very competitive field. We try not to let our rivals know what we've learned."

"Oops, my double-oh badge must be showing." She looked down, patting her clothing as if she were searching for it.

"Nah, you're not a spy. Or if you are, you're not a very good one," he teased. He wished he could help pat her down.

"What's wrong with my spying?" She feigned a pout.

"Well, for one thing, your timing's way off. You said you got here ten days ago."

"No, see … that just shows you how good I am. I knew you were coming even before you did." She smiled in triumph.

Sweetheart, you can show me how good you are any time you like. Doug liked the way the conversation was going. They were playing with words, teasing and getting into the innuendoes that communicate without commitment. "How about a refill? You're down to nothing but ice cubes."

"Thanks, but I think I'll pass."

Shit. She was giving all the right signals. I can't lose her now. "You're not afraid I'll take advantage of you, are you?"

One shoulder hinted at a shrug. "Most sensible women start with that assumption."

Hmm. Straight up answer. She's no bimbo. "Okay, let's assume you're one of those sensible women." Doug spread his hands and raised his eyebrows.

"Why am I here? Long story, most of it not worth telling. I have a friend who's into Tarot cards. She's predicted enough things to make me curious. I bought a deck and brought it with me." She gave him a sheepish smile. "I told you I was bored. Anyway, the cards said I'd meet a T, D and H man. You're not dark, but two out of three isn't bad for a cheap set of cards and someone who can't read them."

He laughed and she joined him. "So what did the cards say to do after you met me?"

"I didn't ask."

Doug slid his chair back, stood, and held out his hand. "Let's go ask."

* * *

Janie's PR training enabled her to "read" people to a certain extent, so she felt fairly safe bringing Doug to her room. Still, the first time with any man was a risk. Was he into S & M? Controlling? Selfish? Janie liked sex, but needed a lot of priming. Early in their relationship, her husband, Mac, had dedicated the necessary time in foreplay to get her turned on, and sex had been good. After they were married, he became lazy, got what *he* wanted, and left her disappointed and angry. She sought satisfaction elsewhere.

Janie had a beautiful body and was not modest about letting a man see it. She enjoyed watching his reaction at first sight. Doug let out a low whistle and shucked his clothes. Janie smiled and slowly turned to let him see her from all angles. He was immediately ready—big, but not *too* big, she was relieved to notice. She resisted his attempts to lead her to the bed. Instead, she directed his hands to her breasts.

"Take your time, big boy. We'll both be glad you did."

Doug didn't need any further instructions. He obviously knew what to do and how to do it. Janie closed her eyes and submitted to those hands with experienced fingers, those lips with a tickling moustache, and pleasure.

PHYLUM

Maria stood beside Alex at the side of the main conference room. The room, like everything else at M-Gen, was over the top, with book-matched veneer wainscoting, a mahogany conference table hewn from a single, colossal plank, and a steel-and-glass chandelier that ran the length of the table. One entire wall was a giant touch screen, displaying the meeting's agenda, with minimized icons scattered across the bottom. Alex told Maria M-Gen's money came from developing genmod seeds. Wherever, Maria could have bought a new car with the money spent on any one of the conference room's furnishings.

Alex had insisted she be there with him, apparently unaware how uncomfortable she was in front of people—and in the room. She hoped no one would ask her any questions.

"Classification of the animal has proven problematic," Alex explained. "Superficially it looks like four tentacles attached to a tiny pyramidal body, but the appendages are not tentacles. Each functions as a gastrovascular cavity and has three eyes and a mouth at the tip. That's unique within the animal kingdom. It's amphibious, spending as much as two hours a day out of the water, and it employs chromatophores for camouflage. Finally, no known phylum has members that manifest tetrahedral symmetry like this specimen."

Alex took a fortifying breath. "We believe it belongs to an unknown phylum."

Doug's head jerked up. "A new phylum? Don't be ridiculous. You've skipped four levels of taxonomy. You two have been smoking something." He scowled at Maria and Alex, and then looked around the polished conference table where a dozen other staff members sat, most clad in white lab coats.

"Why are you arguing against this, Doug?" Martinson, Sr. asked from the head of the table. "This is outstanding! A discovery of this magnitude makes everyone at M-Gen look good. You should be happy someone from your own team is getting the credit."

Doug glared first at his father and then at Maria. She could imagine how miserable it would be to work around him if she received more attention than he did.

"Dr. Martinson?" She struggled to keep her voice from trembling. Even though two other women were in the room, she was the only person without a Ph.D. "I'm uncomfortable with being given all of the credit for the discovery. Alex ... uh, Dr. Goodson saw it first, and Dr. Martinson brought it back from Peru. Can't we share the credit?"

"What a generous suggestion. Doug? Any objections?" Martinson looked imperiously at his son.

Doug turned red, but said nothing.

"I thought not. Very well then, I'd like to make the announcement as soon as possible. Get one of our tech writers to work up a short article. You three decide on a name—genus, species and your recommendation for the phylum. Skip the intermediate levels for now. Get everything to Joyce by noon tomorrow. I want to review it before it goes out."

Joyce, Martinson's executive assistant, was the clearinghouse for everything that took place at M-Gen. If you wanted something to happen, you went to Joyce, not her boss.

Martinson rose, indicating the meeting's end. The room cleared except for Maria, Alex and Doug.

Doug wasted no time taking charge. "All right, let's get this over with," he grumbled. "We've all got work to do. Here's my suggestion."

He cleared the agenda from the touchscreen and wrote *Tetra-*

poda M-Geni with a stylus.

"Well?"

To Maria, it sounded more like a challenge than an invitation for commentary—like he dared anyone to find fault with his suggestion. Alex looked at her, but she wasn't about to aggravate the situation by criticizing Doug's idea. The sooner she could get through this naming process and back to work, the better.

"Well, Doug," Alex said, "it's nice to recognize the company, but using a proper noun for the species doesn't help describe the holotype. The species should provide additional or refining information about the genus."

"It doesn't need refinement," Doug countered. "*Tetrapoda* is sufficient."

"No, it's not. In fact, it's misleading. The appendages are not feet. They're hollow, with a digestive system inside. There's a mouth and three eyes at each tip. *Poda* is wrong."

Maria winced when Alex said the last word. She could almost see Doug bristle. She knew Alex didn't care much for Doug, but never expected him to openly challenge the founder's son when she was present. The last thing she needed was to be caught in the middle of a battle between those two.

"So, I suppose you have a name that perfectly describes an animal with four mouths, four stomachs, and what … twelve eyes?" Doug curled his lip with disdain.

"No, but I have a name that identifies the feature that makes it unique in the animal kingdom." Alex grabbed the stylus from Doug's fingers and wrote *Tetrahedra crucis* on the screen.

"Crucis? De la Cruz in Latin. Very clever. You just said no proper names and then broke your own rule. Why should she get special recognition?"

Maria groaned to herself. That was exactly what she *didn't* want—to get more recognition than Doug. How many ways could he make her regret that?

"Because she's the one who actually made the discovery," Alex replied.

"Wait a minute. She's the one who suggested we share it. *M-Geni* is a great way to do that."

Alex didn't yield, pointing out that the species was supposed to begin with a lower case letter, and a hyphen was non-standard in taxonomic nomenclature. The whole argument was becoming ridiculous to Maria.

Doug started to speak but his cell phone rang, interrupting the argument. He answered it, and the scowl on his face abruptly vanished.

"Hey there … Let me … uh, just a minute." He hurried into the hall, closing the door behind him.

"Wonder who was on the phone," Alex mused. "Doug sounded almost … nice."

"Alex," Maria said, ignoring his comment, "can't you two get through this without so much confrontation? The name isn't important to me. I need to get out of here so I can study for finals."

Alex frowned. "I don't report to him any more now that I have my doctorate. I'm not gonna let him bully me, or you."

"But *I* report to him, and I need to maintain good relations with him. I don't need you to—"

The door opened and Doug came into the room.

"I have to go," he announced. "I've decided I'll name the phylum. You two can name the genus and species."

"*You've* decided?" Alex protested, but Maria shot him a look. "Fine. Whatever. So what name did you choose?"

"*Tetrahedra.* You said it uniquely distinguishes this class of animals from all others. You can come up with a different name for the genus." He didn't wait for agreement or argument. He simply walked out, leaving Alex and Maria alone in the quiet conference room.

"What an arrogant SOB," Alex groused, taking a seat near Maria.

"Alex, give it a rest."

"How can you sit there and quietly accept whatever he dishes out?"

"I can, because keeping my job is more important to me than helping you win a pointless argument with Doug. I need this job so I can afford to care for my grandmother and still do my thesis research without going further into debt. I appreciate you standing up for me, but pushing Doug's buttons just makes things worse. Back off … please."

Her voice softened only slightly as she said the last word. She didn't want to offend him, but neither did she need him to complicate her relationship with Doug.

"I … I'm sorry," he stammered. "I thought—"

"No," she interrupted. "Neither of you were thinking. You were like two alpha males seeing who could squirt your scent highest on the tree." She reddened slightly and quickly changed the subject. "Come on. We've still got to decide on two more names."

"Yeah, Doug stole my name."

"Now see?" Maria pointed her finger at him. "That's the alpha male reaction. The way I see it, he paid you a compliment. He liked your name so well he elevated it to the phylum level."

Maria had spent the previous night transferring the little creature and its flatworm meal into a smaller aquarium where she could examine it better. To her it looked like a miniature starfish, only more three-dimensional. "What if we called it a Peruvian Star?" she suggested.

"That'd work for a common name," Alex agreed, "but there're already too many scientific names with *aster* as the root. The name's sure to appear in all the scientific journals. I want a name that stands out—one that reflects the tetrahedral symmetry."

"All right, what other words describe a tetrahedron?"

"Mm … a pyramid, but pyramids are huge. The specimen is tiny."

"There you go, then. How do you say 'little pyramid' in Latin?"

"I don't know, but there's a book in the library that'll tell us.

Let's go."

Alex made a playful show of offering his arm. On a whim, Maria accepted it. She enjoyed the feel of his biceps flexing beneath her hand as they walked. It was the most intimate she'd ever been with him—with *anyone*. Her stunted arm had repelled all previous admirers. Reluctantly, she released her grip when they reached the hall. She didn't want to start any rumors. So, what, exactly, *did* she want to start?

With a shudder, Maria thought back to the first time she met Alex. What a disaster. He had come to the aquatics lab her first day at M-Gen, introduced himself and offered his hand. She reached to shake it with her left hand, as was her habit, but he withdrew his. "Doesn't that one work?" he asked, indicating her stunted right arm. She was so infuriated with his audacity, she grabbed his hand and squeezed it with all the strength her diminutive hand could muster. He nodded, smiled, and said, "Pleased to meet you, Maria." She fumed about it for several days, until she realized that Alex had only done what she wanted everyone to do—accept her the way she was.

After that, she paid closer attention to him. He fit her idea of handsome—a little taller than her, muscular, but not brawny, with intense blue eyes that drew her in ... and freckles. One in particular on the tip of his nose looked like a crooked smiley face. She had developed an insatiable desire to kiss it.

Maria forced her thoughts back to the present. She could think about him later, when she was alone and had time. Finals were in two days. She sighed and followed Alex down the hall and into the library.

She'd been to M-Gen's posh library a few times before and liked its atmosphere. One wall was solid windows looking out on a central courtyard filled with tropical plants. Water fell from bamboo pipes into a small pond full of koi. She could barely hear the peaceful sound through the glass. Comfortable chairs circled low tables inviting relaxed browsing, and classical music played at low volume from ceiling speakers. Maria recognized Adagio for Strings—one of her favorites. Alex brought a four-inch thick tome to their table and plopped it down, jarring her from her reverie and reminding her they were here for research.

He heaved it open to the *p*'s and then began thumbing the pages. "P ... p-i ... ," he mumbled.

"Alex, give me that!" Maria jerked the book away from him. "It's p-*y*. And *you're* the one with the doctorate!" She raised a critical eyebrow, but grinned to show she was teasing.

She flipped the pages until she found the entry. "Pyramid is *pyramis* in Latin," she said. "Now how do you say 'little'?"

"Greek would be *mikros*," he answered. "Latin is *parvus*. If there's a giant and dwarf version of a species, we would distinguish between them with *gigas* and *nana*."

"Nana? That's it, Alex." She grabbed his arm. "Can we name it *Pyramis nana*, even if there isn't a giant version?" Nana was the pet name she used for her grandmother. She loved the idea of naming the new species after her. "It's like saying Mama," she explained, "except I never knew my mother. Nana raised me. I'd like to honor her in this way if it's okay."

"I don't see why not. We get to choose, remember?"

Alex remained quiet for a moment, then spoke hesitantly. "Maria ... what happened to your mother? I've never heard you speak about either of your parents. If I'm out of line, say so."

"No, it's okay, Alex." It was a topic Maria was comfortable talking about, but she was still pleased at Alex's interest.

Maria's mother had died giving birth to her. Her shoulder had been injured during the difficult delivery, causing her arm to be stunted. She spoke easily about the incident, but when Alex asked about her dad, her expression sobered.

"We're estranged," she said. "He blamed me for my mother's death. That's why Nana raised me. I've seen pictures of him, but never met him in person."

"Wow, Maria. Here you are, one of the nicest, most well-adjusted people I know. Who would guess the obstacles you've had to overcome."

Maria flushed at the praise. "Thank you, Alex. I take back my alpha male remarks. It's nice to have a friend like you." She wanted to hug him—wanted a whole lot more than that, but dared not reveal her feelings.

"Maria, I … ," he began, hesitated, then started again. "Maria, I'd like to be more than just a friend."

His words caught her off guard. Had he read her mind? She felt a flash of anguish before regaining control.

"I can't. No, I … ," she shook her head, "I can't. I'm … not allowed."

"What? What are you talkin' about? You're twenty-six years old, a … a college graduate one semester from your Master's. What do you mean, not allowed?"

"Please. Don't make this harder than it already is. If I go out with you, we'll both end up getting hurt. I don't want that to happen."

She knew this situation would arise eventually—even hoped for it. Why she hoped she didn't know—she couldn't do anything about it, but knowing someone felt that way made her feel good. She stared off into space while she gathered her thoughts.

"I guess the best way to say it is—I've been promised to someone else. Sort of like an arranged marriage. It'd be pointless to go out with you knowing our relationship couldn't go any further."

"Who?" he prodded.

"There isn't a 'who' yet. It has to be someone from a family with pure Spanish bloodlines. Some aristocrat, I suppose."

She told him about the last candidate who had come to check her out. She shuddered with the memory. His skin was pasty white, his hair slick and black. He looked like Count Dracula. She was glad he'd come during the daytime. Fortunately, he'd taken one look at her and caught the next plane home.

"Word has spread that I'm … flawed." She lifted her diminutive arm in explanation.

"That's ridiculous," Alex said, but then his face brightened. "Fine, then. If you're not good enough for them, then you should be free to choose for yourself."

Maria shook her head. "It doesn't work that way. It's a family mandate. Either I marry a blueblood or I don't marry. It's that simple."

"Wow. Maria, I don't wanna insult your heritage, but that's like somethin' from the Dark Ages. Those rules shouldn't apply to you here. You're an American—a legal adult. No one can stop you from getting married."

It *was* from the Dark Ages. Maria's uncles grew up in Spain. Men there still thought of women as property. Alex was right—they couldn't stop her from marrying, but they could take Nana away from her. Nana's mind was beginning to fail, and Maria didn't want them to know. After she got her Master's degree she might make enough so Nana could live with her, instead of the other way around. That was the only hope she had of breaking free of her family's control and still protecting Nana.

"I'm sorry, Alex. I'd like very much to go out with you, but I can't."

Alex fingered his chin. "I want to go out with you, and you'd like to go out with me. There's gotta be a way."

Maria turned her face away from him. "I have to go start my rounds."

She knew her excuse was transparent. None of the animals would starve if she were a few minutes late feeding them, but she felt tears threatening. She hurried toward the supply room.

What have I done? Alex is the first man who's found me attractive in spite of my arm—the only man I can even dream of marrying, and I just turned him down! Why can't I have a love life like everyone else?

CLONES

"Three of its appendages have lost all color," Alex explained. "The cause may be the environment we've got it in, its diet, or something else, but I don't expect it to live more than a few days, if that long. I'd like permission to record its structure with the nanograph."

"Whoa, Goodson," Doug interrupted. "The nanograph is for looking at cells, not entire animals. You'll tie up the machine for days and use half a year's budget recording something that size."

"I don't propose recording the entire animal. It's got tetrahedral symmetry, so we only need to look at one of the four segments. We can make a couple radial slices and a dozen or so cross sections at increasing distances from the center. It should only require a few hundred terabytes, and we can recover some or all of the cost by sharing the data with the scientific community. It might also help convince them that *Tetrahedra* is really a new phylum."

Doug started to object, but his father spoke first.

"Great idea, Goodson. Do it now. I'll have the imaging team waiting for you when you get there."

Alex grabbed his papers and hurried out the door as Martinson picked up the phone.

"Ames ... Martinson here. Dr. Goodson is on his way over with the *Pyramis* specimen from Peru. It's dying. We need to see inside it. Top priority. Highest resolution you can give us ... Thanks."

Martinson started issuing orders before the phone touched its cradle. "Doug, you're going back to Peru. Get Joyce to book a charter flight ASAP and arrange for specimen exports."

"What? No way! I'm still not over the bites I got—"

"Don't argue," Martinson interrupted. "Do it! I'll have the equipment you'll need shipped overnight. Go back to the exact spot you collected the specimen. Try to find more, but your first priority is to define the environment."

"I did!" Doug argued. "It's in my trip report."

"Then do it again. You must have missed something."

He proceeded to itemize the information Doug was to bring back—the water's pH, salinity, oxygen content, temperature … ya-da-yada. Doug let his head drop into his hands and tried to tune out the noise. His father would write out the instructions anyway, micromanaging every detail. Finally, Martinson's attention turned to someone else.

"Winston, as soon as Goodson comes back, see if you can get cells for the cloning process without further stressing the animal. Get help from Hendrix's team if you need it. Consider host cells from every species we have on site."

Martinson was not one to panic, but the fact that he would even consider cloning demonstrated the magnitude of his concern over the potential loss of the specimen—and the fame M-Gen would garner from the discovery.

He barked orders and people disappeared until only a few remained in the conference room. He keyed some notes into his day planner, then left without so much as a glance in Doug's direction.

Doug snapped his pencil in two and threw the pieces across the room. *I'm sick of him treating me like some lackey. Do this! Do that! Why can't he send Goodson? I'm a manager. Send the girl. She speaks Spanish.* He stood and slammed his chair into the conference table.

* * *

After the meeting, Dr. Belleville called Alex upstairs to show him how to extract the nucleus from a cell for cloning. It wasn't until the next afternoon that Alex could report back to Maria what happened in the meeting. He grinned maliciously when he told her Doug had to go back to Peru, listing all the measurements he was instructed to bring back. Maria was astonished. The only parameter M-Gen ever controlled was temperature, using thermo-statically controlled heaters clipped to the walls of the aquariums. She checked the one in *Pyramis'* tank and saw the red glow as the heater element cycled on and off, and she read the temperature on the digital readout, 86° F—correct. Just to be sure, she stuck a thermometer in the tank to verify the thermostat was working properly. When she saw the reading, she sucked in her breath. The water was twelve degrees colder than it should be. The thermostat's readout was badly inaccurate.

Alex relayed her discovery to Dr. Belleville, but by then, it was too late to stop Doug; he was already in Peru. Sadly, it was also too late to save the *Pyramis* specimen. It died the next day.

* * *

PUCALLPA, PERU:
A low bungalow, one of several along a curving dirt path, nestled into its private niche, surrounded by dense plantings of tropical flowers, bushes and trees. Someone knocked at the door, which Doug had propped open to let in the breeze.

"Come in," he yelled from the bedroom. He was stripped to the waist, dabbing his neck with a towel. "It's about damned time. I'm dying in here. No fan, no shower, and humidity you can cut with a knife—"

"You poor thing," a woman's voice interrupted. "Why don't you come to my room? It's just as hot and humid as yours, but the fan works, and you can share the shower with me."

"Janie!" Doug nearly fell over himself entering the room. "Wow, if I'd known you'd be here in Pucallpa, I would've volunteered for the trip. How did you know I was here? And don't give me that stuff about knowing before I did."

"You still question my spying skills? Hmpf." She raised her chin and sniffed. "I told you—the staff knows me now and tells me whenever an American checks in."

She pulled him to her. "C'mere, American."

"Whoa," Doug gasped when she released him. "About that shower … ?"

"Mmm." Janie headed for the door, beckoning with a smile.

* * *

Doug lay on the bed beside Janie, eyes half-closed, listening to the buzz of insects outside the cabin. Janie rested on her side. Her folded arm served as a pillow. The lovers were naked, but not touching. The heat was too oppressive. The out-of-balance ceiling fan wobbled precariously, stirring the humid air. Both bodies glistened with sweat.

"I think I liked it better in the shower," Doug said, finally opening his eyes. "At least it was a little cooler in there."

"Well, we're going to have to take another shower. You can decide afterward which way you like best." She smiled, more with her eyes than her mouth, and rolled to her feet in one smooth motion.

Doug watched the lithe muscles in her buttocks flex gracefully with each step as she walked toward the shower. Suddenly, he remembered he was invited. "Be gentle," he said when the water began flowing. "I have to go tromp in the swamp tomorrow."

* * *

Janie's conscience bothered her most of the evening after Doug left. She had told him who she was when they met two weeks ago, but apparently he didn't recognize her name. Joking about spying came too close to the truth. She should have walked away when she heard his name. *Why do I have such a weakness for good-looking men?* This was going to make her job a lot more difficult. Not enough to break off the relationship, she realized. He was too good with his hands. What a contrast to Mac with his calluses and dirty fingernails!

She thought about Doug and their afternoon together. Most men didn't realize how much of themselves they revealed when they made love. Doug was unhappy. He wanted affection and attention, or maybe recognition. Janie was happy to give him all of those. She'd have to get him out from under his father's thumb to help him, though.

I need to come clean with Doug. This situation could cause us both a lot of trouble.

SECRETS

SEVEN WEEKS LATER:

Doug sauntered into the head geneticist's office with a sneer on his face.

"Belleville, what the hell are you trying to pull off?"

Dr. Winston Belleville jerked his head around at the sound. *Bloody hell! I thought I latched my door.* The intrusion was unwelcome, the intruder even less so.

"It's *Doctor* Belleville to you," he snapped, "and you may also extend me the courtesy of knocking before entering."

"Sure, whatever. I just saw your clones of *Pyramis nana* upstairs. They're like five times bigger than the one I found. Who're you trying to fool?"

"As I recall, *you* didn't find it. The student who works in the aquatics lab did." He allowed a subtle smirk to show.

Doug glowered. "You didn't answer my question. Why are they so big?"

The overweight geneticist let out a disgusted sigh. Producing viable clones from the original *Pyramis nana* specimen had been surprisingly difficult. He had tried every technique in his repertoire without success. Ultimately, he had to bend the rules. It irked him to have to reveal what he'd done, but Doug obviously wasn't going to let the matter drop.

"They're big," he explained, "because if I left them small, they perished. I tried cloning using the normal process. It didn't work. Host cells from twenty-five different species, and not one survived past the fifth division. I had to tweak some of the regulatory sequences controlling growth." His chair protested when he leaned back.

"You what?" The surprised tone in Doug's voice quickly turned accusing. "Did Dad authorize that?"

"He authorized cloning."

"That sure as hell didn't include genetic manipulation."

"For your information, cloning *is* genetic manipulation." Belleville enjoyed rubbing in Doug's failure to become a geneticist. He chuckled to himself, comfortable behind the books, papers, and journals that formed a semicircular mound at arm's length on his desk. He selected two licorice-flavored jellybeans from the bowl on his desk and popped them into his mouth, releasing the anise-like tang into the room.

"Don't get cute with me," Doug retorted. "You know Dad's policies on GM, and you know he wouldn't approve of what you've done."

Belleville laughed out loud. He and D.J. Martinson had been working together for twenty years. Did Doug think his dad would rap Belleville's knuckles? "Are you going to tattle on me?" he asked, still chuckling. "Be careful. Two can play that game. You've bent a few rules, yourself." He stared at Doug with raised eyebrows.

Doug's back stiffened. "What rules? You don't know what you're talking about."

"I'm referring to the time the entire clean room had to be decontaminated because some bloody fool didn't follow protocol. I know who the wanker was."

"I—"

Belleville stopped him with a wave of his hand. "Don't bother trying to deny it. I know what I know." He rested his chin on his fist and looked at Doug through half-closed eyes.

Doug shut his mouth. His ears flushed red.

Belleville had him. He eased his aggressive tone. "I'm doing you a favor here, Doug," he said. "Think what it would've done to M-Gen's reputation—and yours—if we let the only specimen of a new phylum die. You failed to find any more in Peru. Without the clones, the scientific community would question whether it existed in the first place. We didn't exactly open our doors for others to study it." He paused to catch a labored breath. "I'll not allow some technicality to make me appear incompetent. *Pyramis*'s DNA manifests the same regulatory sequences as many other species, including our own. I knew what I was doing."

Doug continued to complain—that the clones had been genetically modified, that they weren't the same animal any more.

Belleville dismissed him with a snort. "You were the one who always pissed and moaned about how small it was," he pointed out, "—how difficult it was to study. I made it bigger." He looked over the top of his glasses.

"Don't try to blame me for this." Doug aimed an accusing finger at Belleville's chest. "You're the one who broke the rules, not me."

"I guess this is what you Yanks call a Mexican standoff. You tattle on me, and I'll reciprocate. We'll both end up losing." He leaned back in his creaking swivel chair. "You keep mum, and we have an animal to show the world. Nobody questions your discovery. Everybody's happy. Look, I've done this hundreds of times with other species."

"Right, and what percentage of the time did you end up with grotesque freaks? You don't know what characteristics you may have introduced."

There was more truth in Doug's words than Belleville cared to admit, but he wouldn't give him the satisfaction of yielding the point. He shrugged, dismissing the question.

"It worked on *Pyramis*. I'll release the first one to the aquatics lab tomorrow. I've got several dozen more in progressive stages of development."

"How're you going to explain the size to Dad? He knows how small the original was. Those clones' bodies are bigger than golf balls."

"Easy," Belleville answered. "We'll tell him the specimen you collected in Peru was a juvenile. He only saw it once or twice and didn't have time to examine it in detail. If something weird crops up, we can blame it on the mitochondria of the host cells. They always introduce variations."

Belleville watched to see if Doug noticed he had switched to the "we" pronoun. It was a trick he had learned years ago.

Doug's lips pursed and he frowned. "Who else knows about this?"

"About what?" Belleville asked, his face the picture of innocence.

"You'd better keep it that way," Doug warned.

Belleville feigned a subdued expression until Doug left, then let a smug smile spread across his face. *Gormless twit.*

The smile faded all too quickly. That gormless twit was next in line to run M-gen. He would be Belleville's boss when the elder Martinson retired—soon, if Belleville had correctly read the signs. Every department head at M-Gen was working on some secret project, scrambling to finalize an exit plan, against the day of mass exodus when Doug would take over. Belleville, too, had a plan. If it worked.

NÚMERO UNO

M-GEN AQUATICS LAB, TANK NO. 27:

<Up, bright light. Down, dark. Dark is good.>

Number One sank to the bottom of the tank, retreating to the corner behind the filter standpipe. The creature heard the sound of the tank lid closing and saw the face of First Outsider peering through the front glass, but the sensations were meaningless—without context. Its universe, up to that point, had been a small transparent container, devoid of anything but the animal and the tepid water in which it swam. The precocial animal had a full array of sense organs, which, up until now, had had nothing significant to sense. First Outsider had provided food during the bright period, it remembered, but also poked and prodded. Nothing happened during the dark period.

<Dark is good.>

Number One remained in the corner for a full cycle of light and dark, cautiously studying its new environment. It tasted the water, listened through its skin to the sound of bubbles rising in the filter standpipe, and watched shadows and colors and shapes move in its field of vision, cataloging each sensation for future reference. Only when the bright lights went out and there were no more startling sounds or motion, did the creature move. It explored the tank meticulously, with only the diffuse glow of a distant light illuminating the way.

<Lightward is a soft boundary, above which there is nothing but heaviness. The current is strong there, and there are tiny things that tickle and taste.>

<Here I bump a hard boundary that I cannot see, and there, and again, there.>

<Darkward I find small, rounded objects covered with food. I can pick them up and hold them in my mouths until the flavor is gone. If I pick up too many, I am pulled down against the darkward boundary.>

It sensed a cycle, a long period of light, followed by a shorter period of semi-darkness. Late in the light period, a new shape appeared—a pattern of black and not-quite white. Unlike First Outsider, this one stayed, moving occasionally, and food filtered down from the soft boundary above. Fascinating vibrations came through the transparent boundary nearest the shape.

Number One no longer hid when this new image appeared. Bringer-of-food was non-threatening, interesting, and inviting of further study.

Four light cycles after being introduced into the tank, Number One's neatly categorized world turned chaotic. First Outsider's features loomed at the front boundary, and the top of the world opened up. Number One retreated to its hideout behind the filter tube, waiting and watching. A shiver of color washed over its skin when a dark shape entered the upper boundary with a plop.

The shape moved with the same jerky rowing motion as Number One, quickly propelling itself to the opposite bottom corner. Number One moved faster yet to put the filter tube between itself and the other animal. Three sets of eyes peered around the tube, and the fourth set searched the tank for an alternate hiding place. Neither creature moved for several hours.

* * *

LATER THAT AFTERNOON:

"*Número Uno, dónde estás?*" Maria bent to see where Number One might be, then noticed the yellow highlighted entry in the open logbook. "Ah, that explains it. Dr. Belleville brought you some company. Come on out. I'll introduce you."

She knew where the star liked to hide, but still had difficulty recognizing the misshapen lump plastered against the back of the filter tube. It was charcoal black with splotches of green here and there, matching the tube's coloring exactly.

"I knew you could change color, but I didn't realize you were that good at it," she said. "And you can control each face independently. That's interesting." She logged her observations in the notebook.

"Where's your roommate?"

Maria pulled a low stool into place, sat, and leaned forward, looking into the partially-filled 20-gallon tank. At first glance, she saw nothing. She examined the plants, then checked all surfaces of the big central rock—even above the water level, but still failed to locate the newcomer. Finally, she found the newest specimen jammed into the front corner of the aquarium, perfectly camouflaged to match the gravel bottom. Only its eyes and trident beaks betrayed its presence.

Number Two adapted to its new home much more quickly than Number One adjusted to having company. Maria enticed them out of hiding by feeding them live brine shrimp, but Number One darted menacingly toward the other animal whenever it approached too close. They had just settled into a tenuous truce, when Number Three entered the tank, and the social equilibrium had to be worked out anew.

Numbers Four through Twelve came spaced a few days apart, keeping the relationships in turmoil. The newcomers rapidly assimilated into a school, but Maria was surprised to find that Number One remained aloof from the others. When one of the stars died, however, she noticed that Number One did not hesitate to join the others in ripping its body apart. Maria sadly recorded in her notebook that the Peruvian Star, *Pyramis nana*, was not only carnivorous, but cannibalistic.

* * *

Number One could not count. The concept of a numbering system might have been within its grasp, but it had no teacher.

Still, it knew how many mouths it had, knew the dimensions of its home in multiples of its body size, and measured time based on the cycles of light and darkness.

It knew it was first, because it could still remember when there were no others, but it did not know the latest addition to the tank was Number Thirteen. It did know this one was different.

Thirteen darted to the bottom of the tank and disappeared immediately, mimicking perfectly the color and texture of the central rock … almost perfectly. Ripples of color washed over its body whenever one of the other stars approached too closely.

Number One knew that sensation and felt a thrill of color flush across its own skin.

<This one is different than the others. This one is like *me*.>

VEINTIDÓS

M-GEN AQUATICS LAB, 3:45 PM:

A blast of unfiltered sunlight flooded the aquatics lab when Maria opened the back door. She paused to remove her sunglasses and to allow her eyes to adjust. The cool air in the lab felt good. She was anxious to see how the star clones had fared since her last shift.

The wooden stool in front of the star tank creaked as Alex slid off. He walked to meet Maria, who greeted him with a big smile.

"Alex, I'm glad you're here. I'm soooo excited! Dr. Martinson agreed to let me include the stars in my thesis research! Doug is not allowed to experiment on them now. Plus, the stars make perfect subjects, since they had no parents to teach them how to communicate. Any communication skills they display have to have been obtained from genetic memory—what Carl Jung called racial memory—the very topic of my thesis."

"Hey, that's great, Maria, especially the part about Doug leaving 'em alone. Maybe that explains why he's so mad."

"He's angry? At me?" The news dampened her excitement. She remembered Alex's warning about Doug making her life miserable. Was his prediction coming true?

"Yeah, I'd say he's angry. He's been ranting all day about your report. He was ready to call you to come in this morning, but I talked him out of it. I remember you told me how hard it is to get someone to stay with your grandmother."

"Alex, I really appreciate your thoughtfulness. I'll go see him right now." She started to close the locker and brace herself for the meeting with Doug, but Alex interrupted her.

"He's not in. He left early. In fact, he's been doing that a lot lately."

"A woman?" she asked, relieved that she didn't have to face Doug.

"Who knows? He prob'ly found a wrinkle and is goin' for Botox injections. He's so self-absorbed, I can't imagine him being interested in anyone but himself."

"Too bad. A woman might help him learn a little sensitivity." Maria made a disgusted face. "What did he say?"

"He said, and I quote: 'That girlfriend of yours has been smoking something.'"

Maria felt herself flush with embarrassment and anger. She'd always been careful to conduct herself in a proper and professional manner to avoid any such rumors. Okay, there was that time in the library when she and Alex were naming the stars, but no one had seen them. Doug's implication that she was some kind of pothead—"smoking something"—that was just ridiculous.

"I hope you told him I'm not your girlfriend," she said, unable to make eye contact.

"Yes. Reluctantly. Much as I wish you were, he's still out of line referring to you that way."

"Thank you, Alex." Maria allowed herself to think about his words. She wished it were true, too. She busied herself to gain control of her emotions. "What did he say about my report?"

"Okay, I'm gonna leave out the sarcasm he put in, but I have to admit I have the same questions he did. First, they're clones, so I wonder how you can possibly tell them apart. Also, why would some of them behave differently than the others? Again, they're clones. And last, you said they've started communicating with each other using the cuttlefish's language? That's quite a stretch. If they can communicate, they'd use their own language, not some other species.'"

His patronizing tone surprised her. Was he striking back at her because she wouldn't go out with him? He had become rather insistent. She thought he understood her family predicament. If Alex didn't support her, no one would. The last thing she needed was a credibility problem. She tried to keep the resentment out of her voice when she responded.

"Well, first, I can only distinguish three of them as individuals. The others look alike to me, too. Second, it's only those same three that exhibit unique behavior. The rest behave like a school of fish. I suspect the three in question were cloned using host cells from a different species than the others. If you can access Dr. Belleville's records we can check. Third, I didn't say they're communicating using the cuttlefish's language. I said they're displaying patterns among themselves *like* the cuttlefish do.

"Alex, that particular point in my report is incredibly important for my thesis. I don't think the stars are just expressing primitive emotions like the cuttlefish. I think they are communicating—at least at a rudimentary level—exploiting a capability they could only have inherited genetically. Humans aren't born with language—only with the capacity for language. I believe the stars have a similar capacity and have begun developing it, but I didn't state that conclusion in my report."

Maria had been studying the cuttlefish for months and was familiar with most of their communication patterns, if not their meanings. Their vocabulary was very limited—perhaps no more extensive than that of crows or blue jays—and primarily emotional. Although the stars used the same mechanism to produce patterns—chromatophores beneath their skin—their vocabulary was much more varied and richer—more comparable to that of dolphins, she thought. Most modern biologists believed that genetic traits merely encoded a propensity to react in certain ways to environmental stimuli—like the cuttlefish's emotional responses. Maria was convinced the stars' pattern displays went well beyond simple emotions—that they exchanged information—*communicated.*

It irritated her that Doug, and now Alex, questioned her competence as an observer. In spite of her efforts to the contrary, she realized her voice had an edge to it. Alex must have noticed.

"I'm sorry, Maria. I didn't get a chance to read your report. I should've known better'n to trust Doug's summary of it."

Learning Alex had not read her report disappointed her, but she felt relieved to know the skepticism was Doug's, not his. She let her defensive attitude evaporate. "Apology accepted."

"You really can tell them apart? Three of 'em, at least?"

"Yes. I'll show you." She started to take his hand but thought better of it. It would only make things worse. "They're a lot easier to study than the original specimen. It was so small."

"Yeah, Doug and Belleville think the original one was a juvenile."

Something in his tone made Maria look at him. "You think it wasn't?"

"I dunno. It's a first—the two of them agreeing on something."

Alex shrugged and followed her to the star tank, where she took a seat on a low stool that put her at eye level with the aquarium. Most of the stars hovered in a loose ball near the central rock. A few had crawled out on top of the rock above the waterline where they typically stayed for a half hour or more each day.

"Okay, let's see," Maria said, glancing around the tank. "There's Number One peeking out from behind the filter pipe. Twenty-two is this one up front, and Thirteen is that one, chasing all the others around the rock. *Hola, Trece y Veintidós.*"

"Bainty Dose?" Alex asked.

"*Veintidós,*" Maria corrected. "*Veinte y dos*—twenty and two. She's my favorite."

"She? How do you know that? The nanogram showed they're hermaphroditic. Each face could be either sex, or even both."

Maria couldn't explain why. Veintidós just seemed like a 'she' to her. Trece, too. It was their gender, not their sex. Número Uno was a guy. He could be very aggressive when the situation called for it, but he was cautious. Most of the time he hung back by the filter pipe and observed. Trece only had one personality trait she could identify—bossiness. She herded the ordinary stars—the ones without any unique behavior—like a Border Collie herds sheep. Veintidós was curious and trusting—maybe not the best combination for her own safety, but it helped Maria. She was almost always up at the front glass, watching Maria, so she studied her more than the others.

"Will you show me how you tell the difference?" Alex asked.

Maria scooted her stool to one side.

"Okay, look at Veintidós. See the thin, beige border at the edge of the triangular faces? Trece's border is more of a taupe and Número Uno's is mauve."

"Holy cow, Maria. Those colors aren't even in most men's vocabularies. I've heard of 'em, but I don't know what color they are, and I'd bet money Doug doesn't either. You'll have a tough time convincing him there's a noticeable difference. Lemme see if I can tell."

Alex knelt down in front of the tank. Just as he did, the star Maria called Veintidós changed from a predominantly black and white pattern to a mottled rusty orange.

"There, that's the problem Doug complained about. This one stayed put when it changed color, but if I saw it here with the black and white pattern and then saw it somewhere else with the orange, I'd never be able to tell it was the same one."

"But you *can* tell, Alex." She pointed out that although the triangular body surfaces changed color, the borders didn't. They were still beige, but even with her help, Alex couldn't see it. They all looked alike to him. Maria tried to hide her disappointment.

"Can you at least tell those three are behaving differently?"

"With you showing me, yes, but I don't think I'd've noticed it on my own. I'm sorry, Maria. You spend a lot of hours looking at 'em every day. I'll take your word there's a difference, and that you can tell 'em apart, but there's no way Doug'll buy it."

"He has to, Alex! These observations are the basis of my thesis. He has to validate them or I won't graduate next semester."

"Why would that keep you from graduating? I didn't write a thesis until I started workin' on my doctorate."

Maria explained that she'd been a pre-med student up until the previous semester. When she came to work at M-Gen, she realized she'd be able to help people better as a geneticist than as a one-armed M.D., so she changed fields. It set her back a year, and her sponsors didn't like it. They said she'd have to write a thesis to prove her aptitude in the new field or they wouldn't fund her next year.

"I can't afford to pay for college myself, and I can't afford any delays in getting my degree. Nana's going to need full-time care soon. That's why I'm under so much pressure about the thesis."

Alex nodded. "I'm beginning to understand what kind of load you're carrying. I wish there was something I could do to help."

"Thank you, Alex. Just talking to someone who cares helps more than you can imagine."

Alex pursed his lips, then paused a moment. "I wonder— maybe I could go get us some take-out. We could eat together and talk some more … if you'd like."

A flood of emotions overwhelmed her. *Dios mío,* yes! She'd like it, but what if someone saw them, and would Alex try to hit on her, and would it be so bad if he did, and …?

"Maria?"

Alex's voice jarred her back to the here-and-now. She smiled a grateful smile. "Yes. Thank you. I'd like that. Don't get me anything, though. Well … maybe a venti green tea if they have it. I brought left-overs from home. I'll hurry through my rounds and be done by the time you get back."

She did hurry and was so excited, she almost fed the wrong food to two different animals. There wasn't much of a place for them to eat, but she set up a folding table and placed a stool on each side. Paper towels folded into triangles would work for napkins. Not very romantic, but she reminded herself that it wasn't supposed to be.

When Alex came, he unwrapped his meal and plastic spork and placed them on the table just as Maria brought her plate of left-overs from the microwave—a colorful dish of rice, green vegetables, and chicken, which filled the air with the spicy aroma of saffron. "Mmm. That looks and smells good," Alex said. "What is it?"

"Valencian paella—sort of a traditional dish in the part of Spain my family is from." She looked at his meal with a critical eye. "What's that?"

"A burrito—sort of a traditional dish in the part of Texas I come from." He grinned.

"Do you eat it often?"

"Often enough. I share an apartment with a med student. Neither of us likes to cook, so we do take-out pretty often. Why?"

"Alex, that single meal probably contains forty percent of your daily limit of fat, cholesterol, and sodium. The Coke and chips make it even worse. If I give you some recipes that are easy to cook and still healthy to eat, would you use them?"

"I guess. I mean sure, but it'd be easier if I just came over to your place."

"Easier for *you*."

"Yeah, I guess you've got your hands full with work and school and takin' care of your grandmother. What do you do when you're gone?"

Maria explained that her next-door neighbor and Nana were old friends. Yolanda looked in or stayed, depending on Nana's condition. On good days, she could manage on her own. On bad days, she only spoke Castilian and didn't recognize anyone. Yolanda didn't mind. She liked to talk whether Nana understood her or not.

No one interrupted them, and Alex didn't try to hit on her. Maria almost felt disappointed—almost. Apparently Alex had been waiting for a green light from Maria. She appreciated that—not being pushed. She enjoyed talking to him so much, she forgot about her worries. They talked … and talked—about money, the stars, their families … . Alex didn't leave until seven o'clock. Maria couldn't remember when she'd been so happy.

FACES

Maria groaned when she heard the doors to the office wing slam and footsteps approach. Coming in on Saturday was difficult enough. She didn't want anyone else in the lab to distract her or waste her precious time. She needed to finish her documentation and get back to Nana.

The steps grew louder. *High heels in the lab? Who could that be?*

"Maria! What're you doing here?"

Doug Martinson appeared to be as surprised and dismayed as she, and with good reason. He had a strikingly attractive woman with him. She was dressed simply, but elegantly—could easily have stepped off the front cover of Vogue. The woman knew clothes. Maria was impressed.

Alex was wrong. He does have a woman. She nearly forgot to answer Doug's question. "I am documenting the three special stars' response to visual stimuli compared to that of the others."

"Can you do it some other time?"

Maria felt herself flush with embarrassment and anger. He was trivializing the importance of her efforts and being downright rude as well. Was he trying to impress the woman with his authority? Could he know that little about women?

"It would be very inconvenient," she answered honestly. "I have to make arrangements in advance for someone to stay with my grandmother so I can come in on Saturday."

Maria's obstinacy caught Doug off guard. It was his turn to redden. He started to speak, but the woman's soft voice stopped him.

"Doug, I don't need to see them right now. It's not that important."

"Neither is what she's doing," he grumbled. "She thinks she

can distinguish one clone from another."

"What makes you think she can't?"

"They're *clones*. They're genetically identical copies of one another." He looked at Maria with contempt.

"Doug, my best friend has twin boys. They're genetically identical copies of one another and I can tell them apart."

I don't know who you are, but I like you. That's what I've been arguing all along. Maria smiled at the woman and the woman smiled back. *I think I've seen her before. I wonder where.*

"May I see them?" the woman asked.

Maria offered her the low stool. She'd never hosted visitors in the lab before. In fact, she wondered if Doug was breaking the rules by bringing an outsider into the lab. If so, it was on his shoulders, not hers.

As soon as the woman sat down, the three stars flashed a new pattern.

"Wups." The woman looked at Maria. "Did two of them just change color?"

"Three," Maria said. "Number One is back by the filter tube. He's harder to see. You're very observant. Are you a biologist?"

"Not one of your caliber. I have a B.S. in biology, but I specialized in botany instead of zoology. I'm Janie McLeod, by the way. Doug forgot his manners." Janie offered her left hand as if that were the normal way to shake hands.

The sensitive gesture impressed Maria so much, she almost forgot her own manners. "I'm pleased to meet you, Janie. Maria de la Cruz."

My caliber? Maria basked in the unexpected praise. *I could really get to like this woman.*

"Janie, you were quick to identify the stars that exhibit unique behavior. I wonder if you can see the same differences in their border colors that I see—the colors around the edges of their faces."

Veintidós hovered close to the front glass. Trece swam lazily back and forth in the center of the tank near the big rock. The woman studied them carefully.

"This one up front has a little bit lighter border. A gray-yellow-brown. A little too much yellow to call it beige, but close. The one in the middle has more brown in its border. Taupe, maybe. I can't see the one in back very well, but I think it has more purple than the others—sort of mauve."

"Exactly."

Maria became so excited she gestured with her withered arm, something she carefully avoided around strangers. The woman did not seem put off by it.

"Doug, you come look, too," Janie said.

Doug stayed where he was.

Maria was well aware how uncomfortable he was being near her, or more precisely, her arm. She was tempted to reach out toward him with it—make him jump back—*or wet himself,* she thought wickedly. Immediately she felt ashamed. Doug wasn't the only one with the irrational aversion. Besides, she needed him to observe firsthand that there were noticeable differences in some of the stars. She moved back to give him space.

Finally, he approached the tank. When he bent down, the three stars changed color again, this time creamy with small blue-gray and black spots.

"Now, see? That's what I have a problem with. How can anyone tell they're the same ones when they keep changing colors?" He directed the question at Janie, ignoring Maria.

"The faces changed colors, but the borders didn't," Janie pointed out. "You have to pay attention, Dear."

The woman stood, smoothed her skirt, and stepped back from the tank. "Men," she said, giving Maria a conspiratorial look. "Thank you, Maria. Come on, Doug. Let's let her get back to work." She turned and walked toward the door.

"Janie—" Doug broke off whatever he started to say and hurried after her, scowling.

Maria sank down on the stool in total amazement. It had taken the woman less than five minutes to demonstrate what she'd been claiming all along. She also put Doug in his place and got away with it, Maria observed, somewhat enviously.

I wonder who she is. Where have I seen her before? Janie McLeod. I don't recognize the name. She's got a degree in biology. Could she have gone to UTEP? Maybe I saw her there on campus. I'll look in my yearbook. She was nice. I wish I could have a friend like her—someone my own age, intelligent, and sensitive. That would be a bit awkward, though—me being friends with my manager's girl-friend.

Maria felt happy—happier than she had felt in a long time. Surely Doug would have to recognize the validity of her observations now that Janie had demonstrated the ability to distinguish among the stars. Her thesis was no longer in jeopardy. She would graduate next semester—one step closer to freedom.

She looked at the three special stars swimming in the tank. They had returned to their most common pattern, a mixture of black and off-white.

"*Queridos*, you sure make things hard for me, changing faces every time someone looks at you.

"Faces! *Dios mío!* That's what you're doing. You're showing us our faces. My colors are black and white. For Alex, you show the colors of his freckles and red hair. How could I have missed this for so long?" Her voice squeaked with excitement.

"Veintidós, do you recognize faces, or are you only duplicating what you see?"

Maria realized she had probably answered her own question. She needed to be realistic about this. If she started claiming her pre-cocious little charges were showing signs of intelligence, she'd have a credibility problem for sure. The idea intrigued her, though, and the satisfaction of solving the color-change mystery left her smiling.

* * *

Janie looked around Doug's office with an appraising eye. Framed certificates, awards and diplomas peppered one wall. A corner cabinet displayed six trophies and a picture of Doug and several other young men holding tennis racquets. A bookcase occupied the wall behind his desk, but held more knickknacks than books. Other than the tennis picture, she saw only one photograph in the room—that of a gray-whiskered black Lab trying to ignore a kitten that pawed at its muzzle.

The room confirmed much of what Janie had already learned about Doug—his desire for recognition, the hole in his life where his family should be, and the hint of a softer, caring side, however deeply buried. She remained silent until they were both seated.

"You really don't like her," she said.

"The girl gives me the creeps. How could you stand being so close to her when she was waving that thing around?" Doug shuddered visibly.

"The girl is a woman, Doug—attractive and intelligent, and that *thing* is her arm, which I'm quite certain is not going to bite you. Not everyone has a perfect body like you do. Show a little sensitivity."

"Like you showed me in front of her?"

"You deserved that. You were being a jerk. Let her do her job and you do yours."

"I don't have a job."

The answer surprised her. Obviously it wasn't literally true—she still had the business card he'd given her in Peru, but it might be the way Doug saw himself—marking time in a job going nowhere.

"You told me you were in charge of regeneration research," she reminded him.

"Yes, Dad insists that I be a manager, but it's not what I want to do."

"What *do* you want to do?" she asked.

Doug told her of his earlier desire to study Law and the conflict his goal caused with his father, who wanted Doug to take over M-Gen when he retired.

Janie nodded in sympathy. "You and I have a lot in common in that respect. We're both strong-willed people with even stronger-willed fathers. I can't work for my father. We'd be at each other's throats constantly. I had to go my own way."

"That doesn't seem to be an option for me," Doug grumbled.

Janie felt certain that with a little encouragement, it *could* become an option, but she hesitated to push him into a situation he was unprepared to handle.

"What about regeneration research?" she asked. "It sounds interesting. Is there some aspect of it that you could do—something you would enjoy?"

"I guess. I liked doing dissections when I was in college."

"Then do them here. Doug, you're unhappy with your life. I can tell. You need to take charge of it. If you're going to stay here at M-Gen, then do something you want to do, and do it well. Start chopping flatworms into pieces. In fact, I have a better idea. Why not be a pioneer and work with this new species?"

* * *

Janie's support and defense of Maria had irritated Doug, and thinking about staying at M-Gen depressed him. He was only half listening. He recognized that she had asked a question and pulled the last five words from that special memory bank that most men develop. Yes, 'work with this new species' was exactly what he would do. It would irritate Maria and impress Janie at the same time.

MOLE

Douglas Martinson, Sr. pressed a button on his desk console. "Joyce, would you hold my calls a few minutes?" He held up a finger for silence until the secretary responded.

"When did it happen?" Doug asked when the console light went out and his father nodded.

"Last Thursday, the eighteenth. Security notified me of it this morning." The fine leather of his chair creaked softly as he shifted position.

"What did they get?"

Doug understood now why his dad had asked him to sit at the desk instead of lounging on the leather couch, as was his habit. He might not know much about genetics, but a security breach, he understood.

"Well, the good news is no technical data was transmitted. Maybe they don't have access to our mainframe database, but whoever sent the e-mail knew most of the dead ends we've encountered in our regeneration research. With that information, Blumenthal will save millions by not going down the wrong path." Martinson ground his teeth together.

"Couldn't Security track the source of the e-mail?"

"Oh, they know where it came from." He explained the message had been sent as unencrypted text straight to Jake Blumenthal at Geneering. Security had tracked it back to Dr. Hendrix's desktop computer, but he was out of town. Someone else was brazen— or stupid—enough to send the e-mail right from Hendrix's office.

M-Gen and Geneering were rival companies founded by rival men. Under Douglas Martinson's leadership, M-Gen grew into a multi-million dollar corporation developing genmod seeds for agriculture. With Jake Blumenthal at its helm, Geneering grew into an even bigger conglomerate funded by the pharmaceutical industry. The "bigger" part had always been a thorn in Martinson's side.

"Damn it!" He pounded his desk. "That son-of-a-bitch planted a mole in our organization."

"Isn't that being a little hypocritical, Dad? You've got a mole in his organization." Doug suppressed an insolent smile. The dig was as close as he dared come to open criticism of his dad. It felt good.

"It's a matter of ethics, Doug. Blumenthal is engaged in industrial espionage. We are not. Our informant merely alerted us there's a leak. Blumenthal stole proprietary information. I hope you can appreciate the distinction."

Ethics, shmethics, Doug thought to himself. *If I went to the trouble of establishing a mole there, I'd use him. That's the way things work in the biotherapeutics industry.* He knew better than to say so. He'd already pushed his luck.

Martinson and Blumenthal had been bitter enemies for years, dating back to the Human Genome Project, when Jake had allegedly stolen Martinson's research documentation and published it as his own. This was just the latest in a long list of real and imagined grievances Doug was aware of.

"What're you going to do?"

"I've talked to Network Security. They're going to modify the mail server to hold any messages going to Geneering. They'll start monitoring all external communication as soon as they can get the software in place. If the mole is unaware his cover is blown, maybe we can catch him next time. I want you to keep your eyes and ears wide open."

"Yeah, right, Dad," Doug scoffed. "I'm the founder's son. When I come into a room, all heads turtle and all conversation stops. I'm the last person to know what's going on in this company."

Doug saw the all-too-familiar disappointment in his father's face. It seemed like nothing he did met his father's expectations—his thesis, getting his doctorate, his regeneration research, even his role in discovering the new phylum.

He shrugged it off. He was going to see Janie tonight. He wouldn't disappoint *her*.

CONTACT

"Queridos."

<Bringer-of-food,> Veintidós flashed when the melodious sound came through the glass walls of the aquarium. The stars had keen hearing. Two other stars echoed the black and white pattern that represented the Outsider who fed them.

<Interest,> Número Uno flashed, swimming toward the front boundary.

<Pleasure anticipation,> Veintidós added.

The familiar shape appeared in the glass briefly, then moved away, going through the motions the stars had learned were associated with food.

The three unique stars watched intently, swimming back and forth against the front pane of the aquarium. Even the ordinary stars took notice.

<Leg-swimming food,> Trece observed, displaying miniature images of rapidly moving prey.

<Chase-eat pleasure,> Número Uno predicted.

<Bringer-of-food. Interest,> Veintidós displayed.

Trece flashed a mottled brown, <disinterest,> then darted at the other stars, which scattered in a starburst pattern of avoidance.

<Interest,> Veintidós insisted, alternating intense color patterns with Maria's black and white.

* * *

Maria opened the lid of the aquarium and poured in a beaker-full of freshly-hatched brine shrimp. Chaos erupted in the tank. Maria heard tiny clinks when their beaks hit the windows, and water splashed out the open lid. More than two dozen stars darted every which way, rowing with three appendages while snatching up brine shrimp with the fourth. Then, the roles switched. The mouth became an oar, another oar became a mouth, and the animal darted off in a different direction.

The Brownian motion continued until the number of brine shrimp dwindled, then the movements became more directed, and competition for prey became intense. Threat patterns rippled across the stars' skin whenever two reached for the same target, and more than one star nursed a bite from a competitor's sharp trident beak.

Maria watched the interactions intently, taking notes. She felt certain the three stars were cooperating, but hesitated to put that conclusion in her report. It would only bring more derision from Doug.

I think I'd better document tonight's experiment in a separate notebook—one that Doug won't see. He would probably say it doesn't have any scientific value. He would be right—it doesn't, but I don't care. This isn't for science; it's for me. I want to touch the stars.

She waited until the stars settled down to digest their meal. If their bellies were full, they might be less inclined to take a bite of her.

The low stool put her face at eye level with the tank. The stars were accustomed to seeing her face, but when she raised her withered arm and wiggled her diminutive fingers in front of the glass, the three stars immediately moved to the front window.

Maria sucked in her breath when she saw the fuzzy images they displayed on their skin. *That's my hand. Those are my fingers. They are communicating! I knew it. I knew it.*

She let them study her fingers, moving them slowly to touch her face, so they would know she felt no danger from the contact.

With heart racing, Maria opened the lid of the aquarium and immersed her fingers in the tepid water. Número Uno displayed threat patterns and darted at the intruders. Failing to intimidate, he moved back to his hideout by the filter pipe. Trece disappeared into a crevice in the central rock, resorting to camouflage. Only Veintidós remained.

The star inched toward Maria's fingers, stretching one appendage forward to its maximum extension with the other three drawn backward, poised to row away at the first sign of danger. Maria noted with relief that the mouth was closed, but it required all of her willpower to hold still while Veintidós explored the skin, nail, cuticle, and even the tiny hair follicles of each finger. It tickled!

Veintidós relaxed from the flight configuration, and Maria allowed her fingers to move very slowly as they had done outside the tank.

"Veintidós, will you allow me to touch you?" Maria spoke in a hushed voice, not wanting to destroy the fragile trust she'd just been granted.

She eased her index finger toward the star. Veintidós did not retreat, but the riot of colors moving across her skin betrayed the intensity of her emotion.

At first, Maria was frustrated. She could see through the glass that her finger was touching Veintidós, but she couldn't feel it. Pushing harder didn't help. It just shoved the star away.

Then something amazing happened. Tears filled Maria's eyes when she felt the star curl two appendages around her finger.

Maria froze, afraid any movement might scare the little creature, but her arm grew tired holding the awkward position. *Dare I?* she wondered.

She eased her hand from the water. The star maintained its grip while the water drained away.

"Do you want to see what humans look like?" Maria whispered.

She brought her hand up even with the top of her head. The star's two free appendages stretched and twisted, turning its eyes in every direction. Maria let her hand descend in front of her body, then raised it close to her face.

Suddenly she pulled it away. "Hooee, Veintidós! Pardon me for saying so, but you stink!" The stench smelled like something in the advanced stages of putrification. It almost made her gag.

The sound of a distant door closing startled Maria. She moved as fast as she dared, lowering her finger into the tank and watching the door until Veintidós released her grip.

Once the aquarium lid was closed, she let out her breath. She felt like a naughty child who just got away with breaking the rules. She knew, with only the tiniest feelings of guilt, that she would be breaking them again.

SUSPICION

Doug sat in one of his father's guest chairs, which was still more comfortable than anything he had in *his* office. Nevertheless, his dad had that this-is-serious look on his face, so Doug dutifully sat at the desk. There'd been another security breach.

"Where is your coat and tie?" Martinson Sr. demanded. "You don't walk down the halls looking like that!"

"It's casual Friday, Dad."

"That's for *employees*, not you."

Doug started to point out that he was an employee, but thought better of it.

"What did they get this time?" he asked, to change the subject. He didn't really care, but he had nothing better to do with his morning. It beat writing reports. Besides, he was curious who was behind the theft.

"We don't know for sure," his father answered, still scowling from the reprimand. "They seem to know everything we know about the stars. That information is not especially valuable, but the fact they know anything means someone is passing on the results of our research."

"If they've got information about the stars," Doug said, "then it has to be the girl—the one with the deformed arm. Working four to midnight with no one around gives her plenty of opportunities to copy information or send e-mails, and she's been coming in on Saturdays lately."

"Do you truly think it's her?"

"Who else? The only other people familiar with the stars are Goodson and Belleville. Could be Goodson *and* the girl. Those two're tight."

Doug chuckled to himself. Implicating both Alex and Maria was a delightful and unexpected bonus.

"Winston is not involved, I'm sure. After all, our mole at Geneering was his idea."

Martinson drummed his fingers on his desk briefly, then picked up the phone. "Joyce, would you ask Dr. Goodson and Miss de la Cruz to report to the Security office as soon as she arrives?"

* * *

"Dr. Goodson, Miss de la Cruz, I am Captain Kierzek, M-Gen Security. You are being asked to participate in an investigation concerning the unauthorized disclosure of M-Gen proprietary information. This investigation is informal. Your participation is voluntary, however a failure to cooperate would be interpreted negatively."

Doug sat at the table next to his father with a self-satisfied look. Martinson, Sr. rhythmically tapped his fingers on the table. Maria sat next to Alex, opposite the two Martinsons. Kierzek, reeking of cigarette smoke, presided at the end of the table.

Maria looked uneasily at Alex. She'd never been in the security office and was glad to have him beside her. No bare bulb dangled over their heads, but the stark gray walls, devoid of any decoration intimidated her and the cold room made her shiver.

"Are you saying we're suspects?" Alex asked.

Exactly what Maria wondered, but never would have asked. For once, she appreciated Alex's alpha male aggressiveness.

"Not at all," Kierzek answered. "We merely would like to ask you a few questions." His tobacco-stained smile did nothing to instill confidence.

"Why us?" Alex persisted.

"The information disclosed came from the project you and Miss de la Cruz are working on," Kierzek answered.

"What about Doug? Is he a suspect, too?"

Maria shuddered at Alex's audacity, but secretly wished she

could have been the one to ask the question. No, she decided she would keep her mouth shut as long as possible.

Doug's righteous expression distorted into anger. "What the hell are you implying, Goodson?"

"I'm not implying anything. I'm simply asking a question. You're the project manager and have just as much access to the information as we do."

"You son-of-a-bitch. *I'm* not the—"

"Doug!" Martinson raised his voice only slightly, but the effect on Doug was immediate. "Sit down. Control yourself. Like it or not, Goodson has made a valid point. I'm not going to have this investigation tainted with accusations of favoritism. You'll be treated no differently than anyone else."

Doug's teeth clenched so tightly his jaw muscles bulged. He shot a look of hatred at Alex that encompassed Maria as well. She shivered, wanting to get closer to Alex, yet at the same time wanting to distance herself from him.

"Very well," Kierzek said. "I'll begin with Miss de la Cruz. Will you tell me where you keep your research data?"

Maria didn't like going first, but wasn't surprised she'd been chosen. She was a woman and had no status. She made sure her voice was steady before answering.

"My observations are uploaded to the mainframe from my laptop. We're also required to maintain physical logbooks. I keep them in my locker. I take them out at the beginning of my shift and lock them up before I go home."

"No one else has access to them?"

"No … well, yes. I submit the logbooks to Dr. Martinson, Jr. periodically for his review." She glanced in Doug's direction without making eye contact, glad to reiterate Alex's earlier point.

"When was the last time?"

She took time to think. "The eighteenth of last month."

"The eighteenth?" Kierzek glanced at the senior Martinson.

"Then you were in the office wing on that day?"

"Not exactly. I left everything in his office at the end of my shift on the seventeenth. It was just after midnight, so technically that made it the eighteenth."

Kierzek looked unhappy, but continued. "His office was unlocked?"

Maria confirmed that it was and breathed a little easier when Kierzek directed his attention toward Doug. Now it was his turn to squirm. She was certain she'd done nothing wrong, but still felt a surge of relief when the man turned away from her.

"So the material was unsecured in your office from midnight until you came in the next morning," Kierzek said. It wasn't a question.

"Wait a minute. I didn't leave it unsecured. She did." Doug looked back and forth from Kierzek to Maria.

Maria felt a twinge of panic. It *could* have been her fault. She remembered meeting her janitor friend in the hall after leaving her logs in Doug's office. He could have taken them. She didn't want to get him in trouble, but maybe she should mention it. She would wait for an opportunity. Kierzek was still grilling Doug.

"You left your office unlocked. Apparently you do that on a regular basis. Is that correct?"

"No ..." Doug squirmed in his seat. "I ... sometimes."

Kierzek nodded and scribbled a note on his pad. "Was the material there when you arrived?"

"Yes. Ask Goodson. I called him in to discuss one of the reports she wrote."

For Doug to ask for Alex's support, he must really be desperate. Maria noticed a tang in the air. He was sweating.

Alex confirmed that Doug had been upset about the report. He had planned to ask Maria to come in early, but Alex had talked him out of it. Doug said Alex could talk to her when she came in at four. He had to leave early.

"Why did you leave early, Doug?" the elder Martinson asked.

Kierzek's grilling had left Doug red-faced, angry, and shaken. Maria could guess how embarrassed he must be, getting questioned in front of her, not to mention Alex and his father. She felt a little smug, but quickly realized the questioning could easily turn back to her.

Doug's answer was elusive—he had to go somewhere, but his father would have none of it. "Don't evade my question. Where did you go?"

"I went to pick up someone at the airport, okay?" His anger surfaced.

"Who?" Kierzek took over the questioning again.

"What the hell difference does it make?" Doug exploded. "I wasn't here when the e-mail went out."

"What e-mail?" Alex asked.

Kierzek scowled at the mention of the e-mail.

"What e-mail?" Alex repeated.

Martinson, Sr. begrudgingly explained about the two security breaches—first, the e-mail that went out on the eighteenth, and later the copy of Maria's lab notes.

"My notes?" Maria asked with alarm.

Alex patted her arm. "Don't worry. It wasn't you." He turned back to Martinson.

"E-mails are easy to trace. You must know who sent it and who received it."

"Yes and no. The message originated from Dr. Hendrix's computer, but he was out of town, so someone else sent it. Unfortunately, we know the recipient very well. It went to Jake Blumenthal at Geneering."

"Blumenthal?" All eyes turned when Maria echoed the name. "That was her name—the woman Doug brought to the aquatics lab last Saturday. Jane Blumenthal. I found her picture in my yearbook."

"What?" Doug screeched. "She's crazy. I don't even know Jane

Blumenthal." His voice rose in pitch with his panic.

"Doug, did you bring someone into the aquatics lab last Saturday?" Martinson's voice gave Maria a chill.

"Yes, but," he stabbed a vicious finger at Maria, "she doesn't know what she's talking about. It wasn't Jane Blumenthal."

"Who did you bring?"

"Her name is Janie McLeod."

Dr. Martinson groaned and let his head fall back against the chair's headrest.

"That's her married name."

* * *

Alex followed Maria to the lab when they left the Security office. He wasn't about to let her go back to work without filling him in on the details of her encounter with Jake Blumenthal's daughter.

"Her name is Janie McLeod," she told him. "I had seen her on campus at UTEP before, so I looked her up in my yearbook. I'd never heard of Jake Blumenthal and had no idea she was his daughter, or that he was head of Geneering. This was just as much a surprise to me as it was to everyone else."

Maria proceeded to give Alex a detailed account of Doug and Janie's visit. When she got to the part about Janie confirming the uniqueness of the three stars, Maria was so excited, she grabbed Alex's hand and squeezed it. She realized she was being forward and let go immediately, but Alex hung on—long enough to make her blush and look down.

"Can I bring my dinner to the lab again tonight?" he asked.

"Alex, we can't—"

Alex stopped her, touching his finger to her lips. "We can. We did. And I enjoyed it—a lot. Did you?"

"Yes, but ... ." Her heart was pounding so hard, she couldn't think or talk.

"Then I'll see you six-ish," he said, and left her standing with her mouth open.

DEMOTION

Martinson, Sr. slammed the door to Doug's office so hard that Doug's framed diploma crashed to the floor. Splinters of glass flew from the broken frame. "How very symbolic. You may as well take the rest of them down. You won't be working in this office any more."

Doug jumped to his feet. "Dad, I—"

"Jake Blumenthal's daughter!" Martinson screamed. "How stupid can you get?" He held up his hand before Doug could reply. "Never mind. I already know the answer. How long has this been going on?"

"A couple of months." Doug's answer came automatically. He knew never to lie to his father. These confrontations came often enough that he'd learned how to avoid escalating them. "I didn't know she was Jake Blumenthal's daughter," he said.

"Why not? I knew the minute I heard her name." Fury burned in Martinson's eyes. Doug had never seen him so angry. This might be a bad one.

"That bald son-of-a-bitch has been sitting there laughing his ass off all this time? Damn you, Doug. Damn you!"

Doug nodded, not to his father, but to himself. Now he understood. His dad was upset that he'd brought Janie into the lab, but what really pissed him off was that Jake Blumenthal was laughing at him.

"Where did you meet her?" Martinson demanded.

"Peru."

"And you didn't think it the least bit suspicious that she just happened to show up while you were there?"

"She didn't show up. *I* did. She told me she'd been there for a week and a half before I arrived."

"Oh, well of course that makes it so. Do you always think with your dick? Do you think at all?"

The earlier questions made Doug remember Janie joking about her spying skills. Surely she wouldn't have said those things if she really was a spy, he thought. She hadn't asked any leading questions … or had she? He had to admit his attention had been elsewhere.

Doug kept quiet. The less he said, the better. He felt his swivel chair behind his leg, but didn't even consider sitting while his father stood. He settled into an at ease stance, hands clasped behind his back.

"What information have you given her?" Martinson demanded.

"I haven't given her any information. We never talked about work."

"Then how the hell does Geneering seem to know everything we do about the stars?"

"That's easy enough to figure out. They've obviously planted a mole here at M-Gen."

Martinson snorted. "Why would they need a mole when they've got you?" He glared at Doug, but resumed the questioning when he got no response. "Whatever possessed you to bring her into the aquatics lab?"

"She wanted to see the stars."

"Then you must have told her about them."

"No, I didn't. She read about the discovery in the journals and was curious to see what they looked like. I showed her. That's all."

"That's *all*?" Martinson shouted. "I've spent years trying to groom you into the kind of man required to succeed me as head of this company, yet you've resisted and disappointed me at every turn. You can't run a world-class research company without commanding respect, and now your womanizing ways have succeeded in making you a laughing stock at M-Gen. You're useless." Martinson turned to leave.

Doug burned with indignation. *I didn't do anything wrong and he's blaming me for everything. It's not fair. He's even taking my job away from me.*

That last thought, more than any of the other perceived injustices, stirred him to action. Broken glass from his diploma crunched underfoot as he strode to intercept his father at the door.

"No you don't!" The look of astonishment on the older man's face bolstered Doug's courage. "It's my turn, now," he said, "and you're going to listen to *me*. You're right, Dad. You've spent years trying to make me into the man you want me to be. I wanted to be a lawyer. No, you wanted me to be a geneticist. Then I wanted to write my thesis on stem cell research. Oh, no, that was too controversial for M-Gen's image. I wanted to work in the labs. Unthinkable! The founder's son had to be a manager. You don't like what I've become? Guess what, Dad. I am what you made me."

Doug let his words sink in, then continued in a calmer voice. "You've made every major decision in my life so far. You may as well make this one, too. You want me to clear out of here? Fine. I'll bet I can get a job at Geneering. You think Jake Blumenthal is laughing, now? Just wait." He shrugged his indifference. "It's your choice."

Doug stepped back from his father and opened the door.

"Oh, yeah … about the womanizing thing. Do you really think no one knows you're screwing your secretary? At least the woman I'm having sex with is divorced. What do *you* think with, Dad?" He did his best to give his father the same withering look his father gave *him* on far too many occasions.

EXONERATION

Janie checked her reflection in the glass façade of M-Gen's building-wide atrium while she approached the entrance. Her knee-length, emerald green suit matched her eyes, hugged her waist, and complimented her auburn hair. *Proper, professional, attractive. I'm here on business.*

The building appeared deserted. Martinson's car sat alone on the front row. It was so quiet she could hear Sunday traffic on I-10 several blocks away.

Dr. Martinson nodded to the guard to let her in, then turned and entered his office. When Janie reached his door, he motioned her to a chair without rising or speaking.

Awkward. I'm going to need all my public relations skills dealing with this man.

"Dr. Martinson, thank you for allowing me to meet with you. Given the circumstances, I was afraid I might not be welcome here."

"You're not. If that's your goal for this meeting, then you may as well leave right now. You said on the phone you had something for me. We're not meeting to make you feel good."

No kidding.

She suppressed her sarcasm when she spoke. It would only aggravate the situation.

"I'm not here for myself," she said. "I'm here for Doug. I don't want him to suffer because of my poor judgment."

"More like pure stupidity," he growled. "What kind of idiot spy would come into our aquatics lab in broad daylight, with my son, no less?"

"I didn't come to spy. Considering who I am, I don't expect you to believe that, but you do need to believe me when I tell you

Doug didn't know who I was, nor has he ever revealed any of M-Gen's sensitive material to me."

"Ms. McLeod, nothing would please me more than to learn Doug was only an innocent victim of your … poor judgment, as you call it. The fact remains, however, information was stolen. You and your statements have no credibility."

"I don't deny information was stolen. I deny being the one who stole it. I had access to the information, and I used it to help me get closer to Doug, but that's all. I'm not your spy."

"If not you, then who?" He stared across the desk at her. "If you want me to believe you, then give me a name."

Janie was prepared to do that, but not without getting something in return. She met his gaze and held it. "First you must promise me Doug will get his job back."

Martinson took a long time answering. Janie took it as a good sign.

"If you're telling the truth, he'll get *a* job back, but not the same one. I can't trust him in a management position after this. You're not the only one who's shown poor judgment in this fiasco."

"One other thing." Janie raised her finger. "My father doesn't know I'm here. He doesn't know about me and Doug, or that I'm going to expose his informant. I'd like to keep it that way."

"Jake doesn't know?"

Janie didn't need her skill reading facial expressions to recognize Martinson was relieved—downright happy at the news. She knew how little respect her father had for D.J. Martinson, and now she was learning just how reciprocal the feelings were.

"He doesn't know because I never told him. If he knew, he'd hound me incessantly to pry information out of Doug. I don't want that kind of relationship."

Martinson seemed to be somewhere else. Finally, he looked up at Janie. "You and Doug. That's got to end."

Janie shrugged. "If it does, it'll be our decision, not yours."

She relaxed. Martinson was on the defensive now. She'd won. Maybe Doug had gotten through to his father during their last argument.

"Very well." Martinson sighed in resignation. "Who am I firing?"

"Your secretary."

"Joyce?" His whole body revealed his shock and disbelief. "It couldn't be Joyce. We're … we've … ." He shut his mouth.

"She made the arrangements for Doug when he went to Peru both times," Janie pointed out. "My father knew almost as soon as Doug."

Martinson slumped in his chair.

DUPED

Winston Belleville sucked in his belly, smiled to the young temp outside Dr. Martinson's office, and hurried into the executive wing hallway.

"Winston?"

Belleville halted at the sound of Martinson's voice and turned toward his door.

"Winston, come in." Martinson waved an arm at the chairs near his desk as he rose to close the door.

Belleville lowered his bulk into the most comfortable looking chair, wheezing from his walk from the parking lot. "What's up?" he asked, when Martinson returned to his desk.

"I thought I'd better let you know I've made some organizational changes that affect you."

"Oh?" Belleville wondered what had prompted the changes and why so sudden. Martinson usually discussed new ideas with him first.

"I've split up Doug's group," Martinson continued. "I put Oscarson, Malone, and Valentine under Hendrix and added Goodson and de la Cruz to your team. You have jurisdiction over anything they do related to the stars."

Belleville pondered the significance of the revelation. Doug didn't have a group any more. Did that mean he was no longer a manager? Demoted? He could only wish.

"Doug is going to be on a special assignment, working in the lab," Martinson said, almost as if he'd read Belleville's mind. "I'll speak more about that in the staff meeting."

Belleville nodded. An awkward silence ensued.

"I suppose you noticed the temp out front?" Martinson pointed with a movement of his head.

"Yes. Not bad," he appraised. "Where's Joyce?"

"I had to let her go."

Belleville jerked his head around to stare at Martinson.

"Let go as in *sack*? D.J., what the hell's going on?"

"Long story. You remember the security leaks I told you about earlier? We thought it might be Maria de la Cruz, but during the investigation we found out that Doug had brought his girlfriend into the aquatics lab. I had to demote him. You may as well know— his girlfriend is Janie McLeod, Jake Blumenthal's daughter."

"What?"

Belleville caught himself in time to suppress most of his reaction. Janie and Doug? Either Jake was a lot dumber than he thought or a lot smarter. What could he be up to? His eyes darted from place to place while he considered the implications.

"The woman asked to meet with me this past Sunday," Martinson continued. "She offered to name Geneering's informant if I'd reinstate Doug. It turned out to be Joyce."

Ah. Belleville nodded. *Brilliant.* "And you believed her?" he asked, marveling at Martinson's naïveté.

Martinson looked defensive. "I'm sure she knew which one of our people was on his payroll."

"No doubt she did, but that doesn't mean she gave you the right name."

By implicating Joyce, Janie had not only convinced Martinson to dismiss his most valuable employee, she had protected the identity of the real agent, too. Belleville watched as the significance of his words sunk in.

"Shit! SHIT!" Martinson screamed, grabbing his head with both hands. "I'm as dumb as my son." He slammed his fists onto the desk. "Joyce's lawyers are going to take me to the cleaners. Maybe M-Gen, too."

"Why? It was an honest mistake. Bring her back and offer her a big bonus."

"I can't. There's a … complication you don't know about." Martinson looked up, then dropped his gaze.

"I'd heard rumors, but I didn't think they were true. What are you going to do?"

"I've got to find out who's leaking information to that son-of-a-bitch."

Belleville shook his head like a disapproving parent. Martinson was the founder and president of a multi-million dollar research center, yet when someone mentioned Jake Blumenthal's name, he reacted like Pavlov's dog.

"We've been mates for a long time," Belleville said. "Listen to me. You can't afford to be thinking about spies. Your number one priority is damage control in your personal life."

He paused as a thought occurred to him. "You need to take some time off. I can manage things here."

Martinson sagged in his chair. "You're right, Winston. Thank you. I may take you up on your offer. I can let Security do the investigation."

The idea of Security mucking around the offices made Belleville uncomfortable. He thought a moment. "Are you sure you want Security involved?" he asked. "Think about it. Doug is dating Jake's daughter. That's about as incriminating as it gets."

"Doug said he didn't know that's who she was."

Belleville gave him a disparaging look, and Martinson nodded in defeat. "What do you recommend?"

Belleville recognized that if opportunity wasn't knocking now, it never would. He considered how he could best profit from the situation. An idea formed.

"If you believe that Doug is innocent, you can put him to the test. Wait until things cool down, then reveal a juicy piece of information to him. If it shows up at Geneering, you'll have your answer."

Belleville pushed himself out of the chair, anxious to end the meeting. "Chin up, D.J. I'm just down the hall if you need me. We'll get through this." *One of us will, anyway. This presents a whole new game plan. Instead of being someone else's pawn, I could be king.*

For some time after leaving Martinson's office, Belleville considered whether to help the incriminating information show up at Geneering or not. He finally decided against it. There was too much work involved, too much risk. Doug was doing fine digging his own hole. Besides, it might not matter. The sequence he'd found in the human genome could make it all irrelevant.

Humans shared thousands of genetic sequences with other animals, but this one was found almost exclusively in animals with regenerative capacity. If the regenerative sequence was there, the only missing piece was the protein that triggered it.

UNCLES

"What's wrong, Nana? You jump every time a dog barks or a car drives by. Are you expecting someone?"

Nana didn't answer. Maria could usually tell when Nana's mind began to drift. She had seemed coherent all morning. Maria let it go. She had to study for an Ethics test. The class had not been one of her favorites at the beginning of the semester, but with the real-life issues she was encountering at M-Gen, the topic was becoming more relevant and interesting.

She'd just begun reading when she heard a car door slam, then two more. The lines around Nana's mouth tightened. She pushed up from her rocker and shuffled down the well-worn hallway to her bedroom.

Maria expected the doorbell, but still jerked when it sounded. When she opened the door, she gasped with shock. Both of her uncles, Norberto and Gregorio, stood on the porch. A third man climbed the creaking steps, carrying a briefcase.

Ay Dios! No! They can't see Nana now. They'll—

"Where is your grandmother?" Norberto demanded, pushing his way past Maria. The other two men followed.

"She … she's resting," Maria stammered. "She needs to—"

"Get her. We have an appointment."

"What appointment?" Maria's throat constricted as she spoke.

"She knows. I called her yesterday. We are taking her for a competency test."

Maria's eyes flew open. "What? You can't! That's not … I thought … You have to have a hearing first." She heard the panic in her own voice.

"We already took care of that," Norberto answered.

His words hit her like a fist in the gut, leaving her gasping for air. She felt the back of Nana's rocker behind her and grasped it for support. They knew about Nana's mind—must have known for some time. What did he mean, 'already took care of it'?

Oh, Dios! There's not going to be a test. They've already taken care of that too.

Maria had known for a long time that this moment would come, but she never imagined her uncles could be so selfish and cruel and uncaring. She tried to think rationally. They must have paid someone off. There was nothing she could do about it, but she vowed to stick by Nana's side no matter where they took her. No way would she make it easy for them.

Maria stood, shoulders back, head high and walked toward Nana's bedroom. She tapped at the open door. "Nana—"

Without a word, Nana marched past Maria and into the living room where she stopped and stared straight ahead as if waiting for a crosswalk signal.

The man with the briefcase stepped forward. "Mrs. de la Cruz, I am Oswald Pinero, attorney at law."

Nana ignored him and the hand he proffered. When Norberto reached to take her by the arm, she whacked him with her cane and walked out the front door, unassisted. Maria hurried to help her down the porch steps. The trio of men followed.

Maria handed Nana into the men's car, then went to the street side to take the other seat. Norberto blocked her path. "You are not going," he said.

He pushed her aside, took the seat himself, and closed the door in Maria's face. She stared in disbelief as the other two men got in the front seat. Gregorio started the car.

Maria sprinted for the house when the car pulled away. She grabbed her purse and car keys and ran out the kitchen door. By the time she backed down her driveway, the other car was two blocks away. It turned a corner and she lost sight of it.

"No!" she screamed.

Her car bottomed out as she tore through the first intersection. She managed to maintain control, but by the time she skidded around the next corner, the other car had disappeared.

She jammed the accelerator down. Six blocks later, she had closed the gap enough to recognize four silhouettes in the car. *Gracias a Dios!*

The men turned into the parking lot of a medical facility. Maria squeezed her Corolla into a narrow space near the building and rushed to help Nana as soon as the men's car stopped.

The staff took Nana directly to a back room. Neither Maria nor her uncles were allowed to accompany her. The lawyer exchanged papers with the receptionist, then took a seat. After another long period of silence, the lawyer leaned to whisper to Norberto. Norberto nodded.

"Where does your grandmother keep the deeds to the family property?" he asked Maria.

Her eyes locked onto his. "You are despicable!" She turned her gaze on the other two. "All of you. Land is more important to you than your own mother."

"We shall see how righteous you feel when you find yourself out on the street," Norberto replied.

Maria faced Norberto. "You seem quite certain what the test results will show. I wonder how much this is costing you."

Norberto started to speak, but the inner door opened and a woman stepped out leading Nana.

Maria looked at her watch. *What a sham. They couldn't possibly conduct a meaningful test in that short a time.*

She darted between Norberto and Nana. "Don't even think about it," she warned. "*I'm* taking her home and you are not welcome there."

Maria didn't attempt conversation on the way home. Lucid or not, Nana's tightly pressed lips communicated her emotional state.

Maria was angry, too, but it had felt good to speak her mind.

She didn't know why she'd been so afraid they'd find out about Nana. Even if Nana was declared incompetent, Maria could still care for her at home with Yolanda's help. All the men wanted was the land. They could have it for all she cared.

Suddenly a chill washed down the back of her neck. *Dios mío! They're going to take our house, too! That's what he meant by 'out on the street'.*

"Oh, Nana," she wailed. "Why did I have to be so impudent? I promised myself I'd be submissive until I could take care of you. Now I've ruined everything!"

Nana remained silent.

REORGANIZATION

Maria sat in the only guest chair available in Alex's tiny office. The sound of footsteps and voices drifted in the open door. Ever since their last "dinner" together in the lab, she had begun stopping by his office at the beginning of her shift. She was ignoring her own advice—allowing their relationship to develop, when it could only end in frustration, but she couldn't help herself. It was nice to talk to Alex—to be with him. She *liked* it.

She had just finished relating the episode about Nana and her uncles to him. He listened, leaning against the front of his desk. "Anything I can do to help?"

"Not unless you've got a few hundred grand laying around that you don't need." Maria managed a wry smile. "I've got to get my Master's and start earning more money. Strange as it sounds, I'm grateful that I work for Doug. He dislikes me so much, he's happy to keep me out of sight on the night shift."

"Mm." Alex compressed his lips.

Maria frowned. "I don't like the sound of that 'mm'. What do you know that I don't?"

"I think Doug got demoted for bringing that woman to the aquatics lab. No one reports to him, anyway."

"I don't report to Doug any more? *Dios!* What if my new manager won't let me work nights? Who *is* my new manager?" Maria's shoulders knotted with tension.

"I shouldn't tell you—I mean it should come through official channels, but you'll be reporting to Belleville. Me, too, when I work with the stars."

Maria sagged against the chair back. It only made sense. Dr. Belleville was the only other person besides Alex who was familiar with the stars, but she knew nothing about him. What would he be like to work with?

"He's been here ever since the company was founded," Alex told her. "He worked on the Human Genome project with Dr. M. back in the '90s. They're good friends. Doesn't care much for Doug, which is a point in his favor as far as I'm concerned. He's a very private person—secretive, almost. I'm interning under him, but it's hard to get him to share what he knows. Other than that, I can't tell you much about him. If you could work for Doug, I'm sure you can work under Belleville."

"It's not that. I need someone to sign my lab notes and verify I can distinguish the three stars from the others. Janie saw the differences right away when Doug showed her the stars, but I'm sure they won't accept her word for it now. If I don't get a signature, my thesis won't be accepted. Alex, this is a disaster! I have to graduate next semester. I have to!"

"Easy, Maria. Don't stress out over it. I'll come eat in the lab with you tonight. We can talk about it then."

Dinner that night was not the pleasant experience it had been on the previous occasions. The conversation topics—Maria's thesis, graduation, and money—were depressing. Alex was sympathetic and supportive, but had no better ideas than she did. On top of that, Alex felt it was time for them to go on a real date, while Maria was already out of her comfort zone regarding their relationship. They nearly had their first argument over it.

"Alex, I told you from the beginning we couldn't have a relationship that would go anywhere. I enjoy spending time with you, and I'm flattered you want to be with me, but it can't go beyond that. Please understand."

VIOLATION

SATURDAY AFTERNOON:

Maria parked less than twenty feet from the lab's back door—a luxury of coming in on Saturday. She was excited about showing Alex the video clips she'd made of the stars and, of course, spending a few hours in his company. She pushed the heavy steel door open, then stopped abruptly.

"*Ay, qué hedor tan pútrido!*" She clapped her hand over her nose. "Alex, what is that smell?" She hurried to the other side of the lab where he was standing.

"I dunno. I kicked the exhaust fans on high, but it'll take a while to clear the room. I brought snacks and drinks. Let's go to my office where we can get away from this stench."

"Okay. I'll be there in a minute. I need to get my laptop."

Maria started to put on her lab coat, but changed her mind. She didn't think Alex had ever seen her in a dress. Maybe she couldn't go out with him, but it wouldn't hurt to let him know she could look pretty. She released the clasp that held her long hair and shook her head, checking the effect in the small mirror attached to her locker door. She smiled at the result, then saw herself blush.

Dios! Why am I thinking about that*! I need to be careful. Alex and I will be alone. I trust him, but now I'm not sure I trust myself!* She grabbed her laptop and hurried down the hall.

"Hey, nice!" he said, giving her a quick top-to-bottom. "There's bagels and cream cheese in the sack," he explained when Maria joined him at his desk. "The drink with the 'X' on the lid is your tea. Venti green without sugar. I think I remember that's what you like."

"How considerate! Yes, you remembered correctly, and I'm glad you brought food. I skipped lunch today."

He noticed! Okay, he just said 'nice', but at least he noticed. Maria sipped her tea while spreading cream cheese on her bagel. The taste was disappointing. The smell in the lab must have affected her taste buds. She wasn't about to complain. It wasn't his fault.

She opened her laptop and brought up a video file. "May I sit beside you?" She scooted her chair around by his without waiting for his answer.

"Here's what I want to show you," she said, pointing to the screen. "These are the cuttlefish in the tank next to the stars. I just fed them," she explained. "What do you see?"

Alex leaned forward. His shoulder rubbed hers, and she rubbed back, feeling uncharacteristically bold.

"Lots of threat patterns."

"Exactly." She opened a second window beside the first and played another clip. "Now here are the stars and *their* threat patterns. Different, right?"

"Well, sure. They're a different species."

"Then how do you explain this?" She clicked a new video clip showing the cuttlefish and star tanks side by side. Número Uno, Trece and Veintidós were taking turns darting toward the cuttlefish, displaying threat patterns. M-Gen's digital camera had caught the episode in fine detail.

"They're teasing 'em!" Alex said around a mouthful of bagel.

"Yes, they are, but they're teasing using the *cuttlefish's* threat patterns, not their own." She grabbed his arm in her excitement. "Alex, the stars have learned the cuttlefish's language!"

"Holy cow, Maria!"

"I know. That's why I invited you here today—not only to show you so you can confirm my observations, but to help me make more videos so I can convince Dr. Belleville."

"Whew. Belleville's gonna need a lot of convincing. I'll help if I can, but we'd better get at it. This may take a while. Let's go see if the smell is gone."

Maria closed her laptop and followed Alex to the aquatics lab, excited about the prospect of being near him for the next few hours.

Her smile became a grimace when Alex pushed open the lab door. The roar of the exhaust fans verified they were working, but with little effect. Whatever had died smelled horrible. All thoughts of romance disappeared. The further she moved into the room, the stronger the odor became. It filled her sinuses and made her dizzy. She walked down the aisle toward the star tank, breathing through the elbow of her dress sleeve. Alex followed.

When she reached the tank she forgot about her nausea. She gazed in astonishment at the tank. All of the stars were out of the water, clinging to plants, rocks and driftwood in clusters of two and three.

"Alex, something must be wrong with the water!"

Maria lifted the lid of the aquarium to check the thermometer. A putrid cloud gushed forth, enveloping her in its swirling miasma. She staggered away from the tank, sucking in a lungful of the fetid air. A dark and ancient sensation spread into her body, impairing, controlling. She grabbed a tabletop for support, but felt her grip weakening. She barely maneuvered her good arm beneath her to break her fall. Her mouth opened to call out, but she managed only a guttural "hagh."

She felt groping, heard ripping, sensed nakedness, then pain. A cry of outrage formed, only to be swallowed by the blackness that enveloped her.

GRIEF

DAYBREAK, SUNDAY MORNING:

This bed's like a rock. Maria stirred, flailing at the sticky cobwebs of the fantasy that lingered. *Dios! How could a dream be so realistic?* Memories of sensual craving and gratification made her blush.

Something else tried to force its way into her consciousness. She eased her eyes open. Bright lights. A forest of skinny, square-trunked trees in rows.

I'm still dreaming.

She sat up. The tree trunks resolved themselves into wooden table legs—tables with glass tanks on them.

The lab. I'm in the lab! Her breath caught in her throat. *If this isn't a dream, then—*

"Nooooo!" she sobbed.

In the corner of her eye, she saw a man on the floor behind her, half naked. His sweat pants bunched around his ankles. She wanted to scream, but she could hardly breathe. He was still there—the man who did this to her! She scrabbled a few feet away, but deep, penetrating pain in her groin stopped her.

A moan jerked her attention back to the man on the floor. He was waking up! What if he tried to take her again? She couldn't run!

She turned, loathing to look at the man, but determined to protect herself as best she could. *Red hair? That's Alex! Oh, Dios, he must have fought with my attacker. He's hurt!*

She crawled toward Alex, overwhelmed by a jumble of emotions—love and gratitude for his efforts to protect her, concern for his welfare, and relief that she would not have to face this tragedy alone.

She reached to touch his shoulder, but jerked back in horror when the stunning significance of his nakedness finally registered.

He didn't fight with anyone. It was him! It was Alex!

Betrayal ... anger ... outrage crashed down on her like a tidal wave. Her mind reeled at the sudden reversal of emotions. She began shaking uncontrollably.

His eyes opened. He looked at her, blinked sleepily, then suddenly sat up. "Maria! I'm sorry! I don't ... I didn't ... I mean—"

"The tea!" Maria looked at him with revulsion and backed away.

"*Hijo de puta!*" she shrieked, "How *could* you?"

He started to get up.

"Don't you move. Don't you dare move!" She rose to her feet, grasping the tables on each side for support until she reached the end of the row.

"But, Maria—"

She reeled to the table near her locker where her purse lay, then crashed into the bar opening the door to the parking lot.

Maria's mind spiraled endlessly as she drove. "*Estoy arruinada. Estoy* arruinada*! Qué voy a hacer*?" She was ruined—disgraced in the eyes of her family—worthless.

"Nana ... Nana ... Nana!"

Block after block the incantation drummed, until the dip at the bottom of her driveway jarred her back to reality.

"Nana!" she cried, the minute she opened the side door. She hurried into the kitchen, struggling to ignore the pain the motion caused. "Nana?"

An elderly woman, wrinkled, but only partially gray sat at the kitchen table, dressed for church—all black. Her husband had died years ago, but at the end of the required mourning period, the attire had become habitual.

When Maria entered the room, the woman looked up, smiled politely, and greeted her in Castilian. There wasn't even a glimmer of recognition. Yolanda came in as Maria collapsed onto a chair, sobbing into the crook of her elbow on the kitchen table.

"Oh, Maria, I'm so sorry. I would have called, but there really was no point. Don't cry, sweetheart. We've been through this before. She'll be back to normal in no time. I'll take her to mass and then out to lunch. You get some rest. You must have worked all night. Come along, Nana. We'll have to hurry if you want to sit in the front pew."

FRIENDS

UNIVERSITY OF TEXAS, EL PASO:

Maria struggled through the motions of life, numb to her surroundings. She'd come to class because that's what she did on Mondays. When class finished, she plodded to her car. She had just opened the door when someone called.

"Maria?"

No! Please, no! I can't face anyone right now. Panic gripped her. She searched for some excuse to forestall a conversation. No one in class ever talked to her. Who could be calling her now? She looked over the top of the car door.

"Janie!"

For a brief moment, Maria felt relief. *It's Janie. I can—* She closed her eyes. Despair returned. *No, even if we were friends, I couldn't tell her what happened. I can't tell* anyone*!*

Maria's Hispanic upbringing was too deeply ingrained. It made no difference if a woman lost her virginity willingly or by force. She was the one disgraced—ruined, never the man.

"Maria, I wondered if we might bump into one another," Janie said, forcing Maria from her gloom. "I also wondered how you would feel about it, considering who I am and the trouble I caused Doug. You may not be comfortable talking to me."

"I … ." Maria's emotions were such a jumble, she didn't know what to say.

After an awkward moment, Janie nodded. "I understand." She backed away and turned to leave.

"Janie, wait!"

The words were out of Maria's mouth before she could stop them, and then she realized she didn't want to stop them. Ever since the day Doug brought Janie into the lab to see the stars, Maria had wanted to get acquainted with her. The timing was awful, but she couldn't let the opportunity pass.

"Please don't go," she begged.

Janie turned again, but didn't approach.

"I'm afraid it's you who may not want to talk to me," she said, hoping to reassure her. "I, uh, had a bad weekend."

"Your grandmother?"

Maria frowned, suspicious. "How do you know about Nana?"

"I remember when Doug brought me to M-Gen, you told him you had to make arrangements for someone to stay with her."

Maria nodded. She *had* told them that, and Janie was very observant, she remembered. Some of her tension drained away.

"I wish I had time to have a cup of tea with you," she said.

"Oh, I've wanted that, too—ever since we met in your lab. I wonder … ," Janie dug in her purse. "Would you like to exchange e-mails? It's not as nice as talking in person, but we can still get acquainted."

A flood of relief washed over Maria. "Yes, I'd like that very much."

Janie handed Maria a business card. "I wrote my cell phone number on the back. It's easy to remember—the area code, then JanieMc. You're welcome to call me any time—or text."

"Thank you." Maria tucked the card in her backpack and scribbled her e-mail address and phone number on a note pad. "I'm sorry I can't stay longer, but I look forward to trading e-mails."

Maria wished she could share a hug with Janie, but she was not ready to be touched by anyone, not even another woman.

* * *

Maria looked up from her laptop when Nana shuffled into the room.

"I made a new friend today," she said. "I just got an e-mail from her."

"That's nice, Dear."

The voice was Nana's, but Maria would have to wait to see if its owner was Nana or just an elderly woman being polite to a stranger.

"Her name is Janie. I want to become good friends with her, but I'm a little bit worried—she's my ex-manager's girlfriend."

"Doug?"

Maria smiled. It *was* Nana. "Yes. He brought her into the lab to see the stars."

"In my day a young man would take his lady *out* to see the stars. Of course there would have been a chaperon—or two. I haven't heard you mention *your* young man recently."

Maria felt a pang of guilt. She hadn't told Nana about being raped. No sense burdening her with a problem neither of them could do anything about.

"I've got exams coming up, Nana. The last thing I need in my life right now is a man."

"Things have a way of working themselves out, Querida."

Now what does she mean by that?

FACE-OFF

Maria entered the aquatics lab through the rear entrance, so she wouldn't have to walk past Alex's office as had become her habit. The thought of facing him filled her with anger and humiliation. She walked to the star tank and sat on the low stool where no one could see her from the hallway door.

When she looked into the tank, the sight that greeted her startled her out of her gloom. Every star in the tank was joined to at least one, and in some cases, two other stars, with their triangular faces aligned and pressed together.

Santos! I think they're mating! Wait 'til Alex sees—

The brief burst of excitement evaporated, and depression returned. There would be no more working side by side with Alex.

You thought he was going to be The One. Well, he was.

An overwhelming sense of loss and betrayal settled over her, pressing her down, until her shoulders sagged and her head drooped. If only she had someone to talk to. Nana seldom recognized her. Yolanda gossiped too much. Janie was nice, but she'd just met her. The only other friend she had was floating in the tank somewhere.

Maria looked for Veintidós among the jumbled mass of geometric bodies. She found her, locked together with the other two special stars in one of the ménage-a-trois formations. Subtle pastel colors washed across their skin like quiet waves breaking on a beach.

"Oh, Queridos, that looks so loving and tender. Why couldn't it have been that way with me and Alex?"

She realized she was talking to the stars while they were mating and felt embarrassed, although the stars showed no reaction to her comment or question. They drifted wherever the current pushed them, tumbling and turning in slow motion, apparently unaware of their surroundings.

Why do they all mate at once? Not a single star is unattached. There are lots of threesomes, as if each star was so frantic to find a partner, it joined with the closest one, or even two. I wish I could have observed the early stages—to see if they have a mating ritual.

"Oh," she said out loud, realizing she *had* seen the beginning— Saturday afternoon when all the stars climbed out of the water. *It wasn't the water temperature. They must have been getting ready to mate.*

Maria tried to remember details, so she could document the mating process. She found it difficult to think objectively. Every observation of the stars' mating activity reminded her of Saturday night. Her face flushed with shame when she remembered the craving of her own body and the gratification that followed.

"Maria?"

"Alex!" She sent the low stool tumbling as she jumped back away from him.

"Maria, please don't be afraid of me. I know what happened … I mean *why* it happened. Someone released an experimental drug in the lab Saturday—that smell—some kind of sexual stimulant. That's the reason we had sex. We—"

"Alex! *Cállate! Oh, Dios mío!*" Maria looked in horror at the open doors leading to the office area. Someone could walk in at any moment and hear what he said.

"Okay, okay," he said, lowering his voice only slightly. "I was in such a hurry to explain so you wouldn't be afraid of me, I … Maria, whatever it was, it caused *all* the animals in the lab to mate, not just us."

"Alex, shut UP!"

Alex pounded his forehead with his fist. "I'm sorry," he whispered. "It's just … I got so excited and relieved when Barry suggested we were drugged, that I couldn't wait to talk to you."

"Barry?"

"Yeah, my roommate."

"You told your roommate what happened?" Maria's face contorted in anger and disbelief. "You callous bastard! Have you no sense of privacy or decency or concern for me whatsoever? Get out!"

She shoved him in the chest, nearly knocking him over. "Get out of here, now!" She looked for something to throw, found only a wet sponge, and hurled it at him anyway.

"Jeez, Maria," he yelled, fending off the missile with his arm. "Give me a break! I was a victim, too."

* * *

Maria sat at her tiny desk, trembling with emotion.

How many other people did he tell? Drugged? Of course I was drugged!

She forced her fists and jaw muscles to relax, breathing slowly. Sex stimulant? She'd been so anxious to shut him up, she hadn't really paid attention to what he said. All of the lab animals mated? That couldn't be true … could it?

Full of righteous indignation, she began examining tanks and aquariums. Masses of eggs stuck to plants, bobbed along the gravel bottom, or floated freely. Water in some tanks was cloudy, and filters were clogged with milt. When she reached the stars' tank she found a yellow sticky note. 'Pls chk e-mail. Alex.'

Frowning, she went back to her desk and logged in.

To: W. Belleville
From: A. Goodson
Cc: M. de la Cruz
Subject: Mass Mating

…

Sight of the subject line made her suck in her breath.

I'll kill him! Her anger returned full-force. *If he said one word about us to Dr. Belleville ...*

She skimmed the e-mail so fast, looking for incriminating evidence, she missed most of its content. The second time she paid more attention and felt herself flush with shame. He hadn't even mentioned they were at M-Gen during the weekend.

His words came back to her. 'I was a victim, too.' *He was telling the truth. We were* both *drugged.*

She sat back down at her desk, feeling whiplash from the reversal of emotions. Alex *hadn't* betrayed her; they were still friends. In fact, he hadn't raped her ... or at least it wasn't his fault. Did that make it okay? No, but she no longer felt humiliated or defiled or disgraced. It was like she and Alex had gone through some traumatic ordeal together, and now they were bonded more tightly than ever. She felt like running down the hall and hugging him. No, she'd said some pretty nasty things to him. First she needed to make amends. She walked to his office, but with a lilt in her step.

"Alex?"

"Maria!" Alex jumped up, almost knocking over his swivel chair. "Come in." He reached out, then dropped his arms, grabbing the guest chair instead.

She pulled the chair toward his desk while he returned to his seat. "We need to talk." She glanced at the open door. "Not here."

"We can go to the lab."

Her hand gripped the armrest. The memory was too vivid to consider going back in there with him that soon. In spite of her conviction that Alex was blameless, the incident still haunted her thoughts. "Do you have any idea who would do such a thing?" she asked.

Alex shrugged. "Belleville's green Bentley was in the parking lot Saturday."

Maria's eyes widened with fear. The possibility that Dr. Belleville might be responsible—even *capable* of committing such an atrocity—had never occurred to her. She *reported* to him! What if … .

"I'm not saying it *was* him," Alex clarified. "Could've been anyone. We've got people with multiple Ph.D's working on God knows what upstairs. Some of them prob'ly even have the capability of doing something like this. Quite frankly I don't think Dr. M. is aware of half of what's going on."

"But you sent the e-mail to Dr. Belleville. If he's—"

"Had to," he interrupted. "If we didn't report it and someone else found out about the mass mating, they'd know we were trying to cover somethin' up."

"Thank you for not mentioning us in the e-mail. I called you an insensitive bastard. I'm sorry, Alex." She stroked his hand.

"Callous bastard," he corrected, "and I deserved it for telling Barry, but I was goin' crazy. I had to talk to someone. How about you? What did your grandmother say?"

Maria looked down. "Nana was … not herself. She doesn't know."

"You didn't have anyone to talk to? Jeez, Maria. That's awful. Jeez. I wish we were somewhere I could give you a hug." He glanced at his office door and then at her.

Maria's eyes misted over. "I'd like that very much."

"Yeah, me, too." Alex pursed his lips, then took her hand. "C'mon, you're taking your dinner break right now."

Maria protested, more from habit than anything, but she insisted that they take separate cars. Alex thought her concerns about appearances were ridiculous, but let her have her way. When she started her car, it went "click, rrr" and then nothing, making the issue irrelevant. She had no choice but to ride with him. They settled on Subway. Maria said that it was healthier than Burger King. Partway there, Alex pulled into an empty parking lot.

"Why are you stopping here?" Maria asked.

"Because we both need a hug and I don't want to wait any longer," he answered, reaching across to pull her to him.

Maria cooperated, wriggling out of her shoulder strap to meet him halfway, but when he tried to kiss her, she pushed him away. It was just too much, too fast. She needed time to process everything that had happened—not just between the two of them, but Nana, her thesis, the stars … the list seemed endless. Alex agreed to be patient, but she knew not for long.

After a quiet moment, Maria looked at Alex and asked, "Why me? You could attract lots of other women—whole ones. Why are you interested in me?"

They sat in the empty parking lot with traffic streaming by while Alex answered her question. He'd gotten engaged to a girl—*woman*, he corrected—a couple years earlier. After the engagement, he discovered she wasn't the person he thought she was. He'd fallen in love with the image she'd projected—an illusion. After that, he was very cautious about the women he went out with.

"*That's* why I'm interested in you, Maria. You're open, honest, unpretentious, and real. You're more whole to me than any of a dozen other women I've ever dated."

With tears streaming down her face, Maria leaned over and kissed him, allowing him all the time he wanted to kiss her back.

After a long, luxurious sigh, she asked, "Can we go eat now? I need to get back in time to figure out what's wrong with my car."

The problem turned out to be a dead battery, which Alex insisted on using as an excuse to take Maria home at the end of her shift. Nana was asleep, but Alex got to meet Maria's neighbor, Yolanda, who looked after Nana when Maria was gone. Yolanda wiggled her eyebrows and made thumbs up gestures of approval to Maria behind Alex's back. A *doctor*! Maria expected Yolanda would spread the word to everyone in El Paso by morning.

JEOPARDY

Maria had finally built up enough courage to confront the only two people who could validate her thesis notes. The scholarship sponsors said it had to be her manager or the department head—Doug or Dr. Belleville. Maria was afraid of Dr. Belleville. Ever since she learned that he might be the culprit who released the drugs in the lab the night of the mass mating, she'd lost her trust in him. Nevertheless, he'd always been respectful toward her—whether sincere or feigned, so she had asked him to set up the meeting in his office.

His office brought the term "organized chaos" to her mind. Every horizontal surface was stacked with teetering piles of papers and journals. Maria smelled anise, but couldn't identify the source, until Belleville popped a black jellybean into his mouth.

"Doug," Belleville said, leaning back in his chair. "Maria here tells me your lady friend could see differences in three of the stars. Are you willing to attest to that and sign her lab notes?" That was Belleville's way—get straight to the point.

Doug flicked a speck of dust from his tie. "Maybe she could, maybe she couldn't, but I can't. I'm not signing anything unless I can observe it myself."

Belleville gave Maria a sympathetic look. "I concur with Doug's policy, Maria. You're the only one at M-Gen to have reported unique behavior and markings among the stars. I won't say you're wrong, but due to the highly subjective nature of your claim, I, too, must withhold my endorsement."

"Good," Doug growled. "Now Dad doesn't have any reason to keep me from experimenting on them."

The men's words hit Maria like a medicine ball. Not only would she get an incomplete for the semester, but Doug would likely repeat the atrocities he committed with the starfish, only this time the stars would be his victims. She left Belleville's office as quickly as she could. She refused to let Doug have the satisfaction of seeing her cry.

* * *

"Hell will freeze over before I'll do her any favors," Doug said after she left.

"Why the animosity?" Belleville asked, then nodded his head. "Ahh … did she have something to do with your … um … change of status?"

Belleville could hardly keep himself from laughing out loud. Thanks to Doug's making a fool of himself, Belleville was almost guaranteed to succeed the senior Martinson as head of M-Gen. He'd have to find some subtle way to reward Maria for exposing Doug.

"She's going to be very sorry," Doug predicted, bringing Belleville back to reality. "I've got a nice surprise for her."

Belleville raised his eyebrows. "She reports to me now, Doug. Founder's son or not, I won't tolerate you harassing her with your petty acts of vengeance."

"You're *defending* her?" Doug's voice rose to a squeak. "The girl's hallucinatory."

"No, it only took her a few minutes to demonstrate to me she can uniquely identify some of the stars. Her claim is valid."

"Then why don't *you* sign her notes?" he demanded.

"You know bloody well why."

Maria was writing her thesis on *Pyramis nana*, but the clones were not *Pyramis nana*. They'd been engineered. If that fact ever surfaced, Belleville didn't want his signature on any of her papers. He would completely lose credibility among his peers in academia.

"How could anyone find out? You and I are the only two who know about the genetic manipulation."

"Yes, well, one of us is a wally when it comes to security issues."

Doug reddened but didn't respond.

"You stick to your new job, whatever that is," Belleville instructed. "Leave Maria alone."

"Don't worry. The less I see of her, the better. I'm going to be doing exactly what Dad and I agreed on—regeneration experiments. And since the stars are no longer off limits, I'm going to make damned sure the first one I cut up is one of her favorites."

ALPHABET

A ribbon of algae curled away from the scraper blade as Maria cleaned the front glass of the aquarium. A fight broke out among the stars, each trying to make off with a chunk of the tasty food. The three unique stars managed to get more than their share by teaming up against the others.

Once the window was clean, Maria waited for the stars to settle into their accustomed places—Veintidós near the front, Número Uno by the filter pipe, and Trece by the central rock. The ordinary stars clustered into an amorphous blob in the right half of the aquarium.

Maria felt her excitement growing. The experiment was the most important of any she had conducted to date. The stars had been reflecting the staff's face and hair coloring ever since their introduction into the tank. Maria wanted to know if they could reproduce an image from memory. She turned on the hood light and adjusted the video camera to focus on the area in front of the rock.

Maria sat down in front of the tank with a stack of flash cards in her lap. She held the first card where Veintidós could see it and spoke clearly. "A." She knew the stars could sense vibrations with their skin, but wasn't sure if they could discern the subtleties of human speech.

A lump formed in her throat when a black-and-white pattern formed on the star's skin. Three ragged copies of the letter, A, were displayed, one in each corner of the star's triangular face. Veintidós slowly rolled clockwise, but the letters remained upright, like bucket seats on a three-armed Ferris wheel.

Maria lowered the card and replaced it with the next one. "B," she said.

Veintidós duplicated the letter's shape. Maria repeated the process for *C*. After four repetitions, she placed the cards in her lap.

With fingers crossed, she called out the first letter, "*A*."

A thrill coursed through her body when three imperfect, but recognizable *A*'s appeared on the star's face. "*B*," Maria said. The letters looked more like figure eights, but there was no question the star remembered the image and associated it with the sound. The set of *C*'s was the most legible.

"Oh, Veintidós, I knew you could do it. I just knew it!" Maria wanted to reach into the tank and hug Veintidós. She realized she'd have to be careful. Her fondness for the stars might taint her objectivity.

"Veintidós, I don't expect you to learn all of the letters, but I'll show you how we humans learn our *a-b-c*'s. I'll flash the cards while I sing."

Maria began singing the children's alphabet song, flipping the flash cards as she sang each letter. When she finished the song, Veintidós erupted in an aurora of color. Número Uno and Trece immediately swam to the front. Maria wondered if Veintidós had called them.

Then she knew.

Veintidós began displaying the letters of the alphabet to the other two stars. Número Uno and Trece duplicated the patterns, but apparently not to Veintidós' satisfaction. She repeated the displays until they got them right. She was teaching them their *a-b-c*'s!

Maria trembled from the enormity of her discovery. *They can memorize, associate abstract symbols with sounds, grasp the concept of sequence, even teach! What else can they do?*

She nearly panicked. *Dios! What if Doug starts experimenting on the stars? I have to tell Alex. No. Telling him won't work. He'll never believe me. I hardly believe it myself. I have to show him.*

She glanced at her watch. *After eleven. Too late. I've got to get home to Nana. Tomorrow. I'll show him as soon as I get to work.*

She looked up to see three stars waiting at the front glass. Veintidós began the sequence of letters and made it to *G* with no mistakes.

Maria's hand shook when she picked up the flash cards again.

"*A*," she said.

CHOP-CHOP

Doug felt in such a good mood he actually greeted the people he passed in the hall. Only Alex and Maria knew about the security debacle, and they didn't know his father had demoted him. The news of Joyce's termination was such a hot topic, the announcement of his special assignment drew minimal attention. He was free of managerial responsibilities and looking forward to some hands-on lab work.

Janie was right. I've been trying to satisfy Dad for so long, I've forgotten what it feels like to do something I want to do. It's time to start doing things that satisfy me. Dad should never have made me a manager. I don't have people skills ... except the kind Janie likes. He chuckled.

He whistled tunelessly while he pushed a stainless steel cart through the door of the aquatics lab. The cart held an assortment of beakers, test tubes, scalpels, spatulas, calipers and scales—equipment he would need for the regeneration experiments. He parked the cart beside the star tank and peered through the front glass.

Three of the stars changed to a lighter color as soon as his face neared the tank. Although he'd never admit it, Doug knew Maria was right about those three exhibiting unique behavior, but he truly believed it was her imagination that she could distinguish among them. He certainly couldn't.

"Thanks, guys," he said, addressing the three stars. "I'll get to you later. I'm going to practice on one of your buddies, first."

He took a dip net from the cart and opened the lid of the aquarium. As soon as the net entered the water, the stars disappeared, camouflaged as gravel, plants or rock.

Doug scooped deep enough to pick up some of the gravel.

He couldn't see the stars, but he hoped to get one or two in the net. When he lifted the net, he knew he had one. It tried to duplicate the woven green pattern of the net, but succeeded only in matching the color.

Doug emptied the net onto a flat pan, then put on a pair of rubber gloves. As soon as he touched the star, all four of its appendages retracted into its body and expelled a dark brown fluid. He collected as much fluid as he could with an eyedropper and stored it in a test tube, then he measured the star with calipers and scales, recording the information in a notebook.

A beak and three eyes ventured out, but jerked back when Doug moved.

"Ready or not, here I come," he warned.

He held the star down with his thumb and finger, squeezed until an appendage popped out, and cut it off with a scalpel. Vivid colors flashed across the injured animal's skin, while the severed part turned ashen. A small amount of brown-red blood oozed from both cut surfaces, then stopped.

Doug dipped a beaker into the tank and transferred water into two containers. With a spatula he scooped up the animal and its severed appendage, placing each in a separate vessel. He studied both containers, jotting notes in his book.

"Okay," he said, turning to the tank. "Who's next? It may as well be one of you," addressing the three stars which now flashed deep red and black striped patterns.

One of them backed into the top front corner of the aquarium. It would be too difficult to catch it with the net. If it didn't move, he thought he could pin it against the tank frame with his fingers and cut it at the same time.

He picked up the scalpel, poised both hands above the water, and grabbed. He saw the star's skin flashing colors between his fingers. He had it. He quickly sliced off a corner of the body with its attached appendage.

* * *

The screams carried all the way to the front lobby. Bewildered and frightened faces appeared in office doorways. Several people ran toward the aquatics lab as the screaming continued.

Doug lay on the floor, writhing in pain. The glove on his right hand was chewed into tatters. Dark brown fluid and bright red blood oozed from a dozen holes in his skin. He clawed at his hand to scrape away two stars whose beaks were still impaled in his flesh, but passed out before succeeding.

ATTACK

Maria pulled to the side of the road when an ambulance approached, siren wailing. Two cars passed her, ignoring the oncoming vehicle.

Did that come from M-Gen? I hope not. I don't need anything else to worry about. She drove on, worrying anyway. When she reached the M-Gen security gate, she swiped her ID and found a parking spot near the building.

As soon as she opened the lobby door, she knew something was wrong. Both doctors from M-Gen's infirmary were in Dr. Martinson's office. People stood in small knots, talking and gesturing. "What happened?" she asked.

"Those clone things attacked somebody. He was hurt so badly they had to take him to the hospital."

Maria sucked in her breath. "The stars? *Dios mío!*"

She dodged people as she charged down the hall, trying to imagine how the stars could be involved. How could they have gotten out of their aquarium? There had to be a mistake.

Alex was standing at the entrance to the aquatics lab. She ran to him. "Alex! Thank God it wasn't you. They said the stars attacked someone."

"Maria!" Alex stepped in front of her. "Don't go in there. You don't want to see it."

"See what? Who did the stars attack? How could they attack anyone? Are they sure it was the stars?"

"Slow down, Maria. We don't know exactly what happened. It was Doug. It looks like he cut two stars for a regeneration experiment. Parts of one star were in containers on his cart. He must've gone back to the tank to get another star when they attacked. We found him on the floor. His hand's badly mangled."

"He cut two of the stars? Which ones?" She struggled to get past him. "Alex, let me by. I have to see." She pushed her way through the doorway and ran to the row containing the star tank.

"Nooooooo!" Her wail echoed down the hall. "Not Veintidós," she sobbed. "Alex, he cut Veintidós."

* * *

The injured star pressed its severed appendage into the corner of the aquarium, while incoherent splotches of color swirled over its skin. Número Uno and Trece took up defensive positions between Veintidós and the other stars, which were clustered so tight, they appeared like a roiling bundle of worms.

Deep red-brown stripes raced from the center of Trece's faces to the tips of her appendages. The color darkened almost to black, and the space between the stripes narrowed to such a point, it looked like bolts of forked lightning moving across a threatening sky.

Trece didn't need human words to express her emotions.

<Outsiders danger,> she flashed. <Outsiders enemy. Bite outsiders! Bite outsiders!>

* * *

Maria and Alex walked toward Belleville's office together. She was so angry, she could hardly speak. "He *promised*, Alex! Dr. Martinson gave me his word there would be no experiments on the stars until I finished my thesis. He broke his promise."

"Maria, you don't know that for sure. Maybe Doug did it in defiance of Dr. M's orders. I think somethin' happened between the two of them right before the reorg."

Maria considered the possibility. Alex might be right about it being Doug's idea. He could have done it in retaliation for her tattling on him when he brought Janie into the lab. That made her feel angry again and then guilty. Had her action indirectly caused the stars' suffering?

There wasn't time to worry about it now. They'd reached Belleville's office. They went in and took seats. Maria felt safe with Alex beside her. Belleville began talking without preamble.

"I called you two in together because I'm short on time," he said. "I'll be filling in for Dr. Martinson the rest of the week, perhaps longer. He'll be staying at the hospital until Doug's out of danger. Goodson, you're in charge of the stars. Maria you report to him. Neither of you is to open the lid of the tank for any reason unless the other is there with you. Understood?"

Maria nodded. "I understand, but—"

"No *but*'s. The founder's son is hospitalized because of those stars. No matter how much you trust them, we'll not chance another accident. Now can you follow instructions, or must I take you off this project?"

"No sir … I mean yes, sir, I'll follow your instructions."

"Very well. I'll share what little I know." Belleville shifted in his chair before continuing. "Based on the nature of Doug's wounds, it seems the stars' bite would be more accurately termed a sting. They pierce the flesh with their beaks, then inject the contents of their stomachs into the wound. That's the dark brown fluid we found in the test tube. It's nasty stuff—a mixture of digestive juices and food in various stages of decomposition. Doug has a necrotizing infection of the ligaments the doctors can't seem to neutralize. The prognosis is not good. It's likely he'll lose his hand."

"*Ay Dios!*" Maria whispered.

At the time, she had felt a sense of righteous justice when she learned the stars had bitten Doug, but to *lose* his hand? She, more than anyone, knew what that meant. Her stunted arm prickled in sympathy—or was it just an itch? She rubbed it and hurried to catch Alex in the hall.

EXPECTATIONS

Rain swept in sheets across the parking lot when Maria cleared the security gate. She drove back and forth, row after row looking for a spot close to the building. Nothing. She was going to get soaked.

She took off her shoes and tucked them under her stunted arm, cracked open the car door, and stuck her umbrella up through the opening. "Please open," she begged when she swung her legs out and pressed the release button on the umbrella.

It opened with a pop and flew away, ripped from her grasp by a gust of wind that sent it sailing and cartwheeling across the parking lot.

Dumfounded, she watched it disappear, until a bolt of lightning sent her running for the back entrance. She stepped through the door, breathless and drenched.

Alex hurried toward her from the front of the lab. "Maria, you're sopping wet."

She covered herself with her good arm, knowing her blouse and bra were soaked and nearly transparent. She looked at Alex in embarrassment, her hair plastered against her face and water dripping from her clothes.

"Wait here," he said. "I'll get you some towels from the fitness center."

Maria had her locker open when Alex returned. "Where is my other shoe? Don't tell me I dropped it out in the parking lot. Those flats were brand new!" She grabbed a towel from Alex, crammed it hard against her mouth, and screamed as loud as she could. "What else can go wrong with my life?" she asked in frustration, combing wet hair from her face with her fingers. She knew one answer to that question, but shoved the possibility to the back of her mind. It was too early to tell, anyway.

She dabbed her face dry with the towel. "I'll be back." She took the towels and her lab coat, limped one-shoed to the restroom, and shut herself in one of the stalls. She stripped, except for her panties, which were only damp, dried herself off, and put on the coat.

Back in the lab, she hung her wet clothes in her locker along with her lone shoe and went to join Alex in front of the star tank. She felt both naughty and sexy being so close to him barefoot and braless. She hoped he wouldn't notice her blush. At least she wasn't afraid of him any more. They were back to being friends again. *More* than friends, Maria thought with a smile, remembering their first kiss in the parking lot on the way to Subway. They were like first-time lovers not sure what to do next.

"What's going on?" Alex asked. "Want to talk about it?" He leaned against the tabletop and pulled a stool close for her. She slid onto it, smiling her thanks.

"Oh, you already know most of it. It's just too many things all at once. What happened to us, my thesis disaster, Veintidós and Doug, Nana, plus something's going on with my bad arm."

"What's wrong with it?"

"I don't know. It's puffy and a little pink." She lifted her arm for him to see. "It itches."

"Why don't you go to the infirmary? We've got state-of-the-art equipment here, and the doctors sit around readin' medical journals most of the time."

"Oh, that's a good idea. Thanks. It'll save me having to take time off to go to a doctor's office. Uh … I need to get there before they close at five. Will you wait?"

She squeezed his arm as she asked. "I've got something really exciting to talk to you about the stars."

"Sure, I'm not going anywhere until the rain lets up."

* * *

"Wow," Maria said, returning from the infirmary. "What a pleasant experience—no sitting and waiting while sick people breathed on me. Two doctors almost fought over me.

"The doctor didn't find anything wrong. She said the pink color didn't look like an inflammation or rash, but she took some blood samples. I'll get the results tomorrow or the next day."

Alex rotated his head slowly, inhaling. "Do you smell somethin'?"

Maria gasped. "Alex! Please don't say that. Are you serious?" She began edging away from him.

"No, no," he hurried to assure her. "Nothing like *that* smell. Nice, like … rosemary—some spice. I thought you might be wearing perfume."

Maria relaxed after the scare. She didn't smell anything. She rarely wore perfume and wouldn't have chosen rosemary if she did. Veintidós' condition was her number one priority right now. "How is she?" she asked.

"Good," Alex said. "In fact, very good. It's only been two days, and the wound's closed up already. There's new growth around the edges. The same thing's happenin' with the other star that Doug cut. They're regenerating."

"Uh oh." Maria compressed her lips. She wasn't sure how happy she was about that news. She wanted Veintidós to recover, but definitely didn't want the stars to become guinea pigs for regeneration research. Ever since Doug cut Veintidós, Trece had begun flashing threat patterns at Maria and Número Uno stayed in his spot back by the filter tube. Even Veintidós showed her reluctance to approach the front glass.

"Maria, you need to be realistic about your expectations," Alex argued. "Regeneration research is a big part of what M-Gen does. You've become attached to the stars, and I understand your feelings, but to everyone else at M-Gen, they're just lab animals. It could happen again. Doug's due back at work any day now."

Alex's words stunned Maria, not only the shocking truth of his statement, but the possibility that he numbered among the 'everyone else' who thought of the stars as mere lab animals. *Every time I think Alex shares my views, he does or says something to make me wonder.*

"Alex, I believe my expectations are quite reasonable." She looked straight at him. "Regeneration research should not involve chopping animals into pieces. It's been done thousands of times and thoroughly documented. There's absolutely no justification for doing it again. I've said it before—this is a genetic research company. We should be researching genes—looking for genetic sequences related to regeneration, then finding the same sequence in the human genome to see if it can be activated."

"Maria, I don't disagree with you. That's a perfectly reasonable approach, but I'll stick with what I said. It's not realistic. When people throw a live lobster into a pot of boiling water, they don't sympathize. They salivate. That's the nature of the beast that calls itself human, and it's not gonna change. Whether it's for pleasure, convenience or the good of mankind or whether the subject's a flatworm, a lab rat or a fellow human, in most people's minds, the end justifies the means."

Not in her mind. She wasn't a moral absolutist, nevertheless, too many atrocities had been justified using the for-the-greater-good excuse. Still, Alex was right. She wasn't being realistic. Even if she convinced everyone of the stars' intelligence, it wouldn't stop them from performing experiments on them. It would more likely have the opposite effect. They must be protected. Whether she loved Alex or not, Maria didn't know if she could count on him to help her now or trust him with her discovery. It was going to be up to her.

Alex's words echoed in her mind after he left. *'Doug's due back at work any day now.'* She had to figure something out, and fast.

Of all the ideas that occurred to her, only one persisted—

hide the stars. *No one but me can tell them apart. Would anyone notice three were missing? I could hide them at home. That would be stealing. Does the end justify the means?*

Her stomach churned along with her conscience.

DESTRUCTION

Doug flopped down into his office chair. The new girl's synthetic, suck-up greeting had irritated him. He would have come in the rear entrance to avoid her, but he wasn't ready to face the aquatics lab yet. His arm ached. Wearing the sling helped, but the most comfortable position put his bandaged stump up where everyone would notice it. He just wanted to be left alone.

Word of his return spread throughout the facility. A stream of well-wishers stopped by his office, but the welcoming turned disastrous when more than one visitor remembered too late that he couldn't shake hands. By mid-morning, Doug was in a vile mood, angry, and full of self-pity. He barged into his father's office and threw himself onto the leather recliner.

"I want those stars destroyed," he said. "They're too dangerous to keep in our lab."

Dr. Martinson frowned. "Yes, they're dangerous, and we didn't know it, but that's why we have research protocols when dealing with a new animal species. You paid a terrible price for your mistake, and I understand your feelings, but I don't want to be hasty about destroying the stars. The consequences of such a decision need to be thought out."

"What's to think about? They have no scientific or economic value. The journals refuse to recognize the new phylum, thanks to whoever leaked the news of the clones to the media."

"Be that as it may, the regeneration experiment you started is showing positive results. The stars regenerate much more rapidly than any other species we've tested."

"So what? There are plenty of other animals with regeneration capability. You still don't know how to capitalize on it."

"That's exactly why I want you back as regeneration manager—to find out how they do it and if we can give that capability to humans."

Doug shook his head in disgust. "You just don't get it, do you, Dad? I told you before my accident I didn't want to be a manager, and I'm not going to be one."

"That isn't your decision to make," Martinson snapped. "I'm sure as hell not paying you six figures to cut tails off lizards."

"It *is* my decision, and I've already made it. Keep the damned stars for all I care. Let them bite someone else. Get sued. I'm out of here. I'm going back to school to study law."

"Law! That crazy idea again?"

"Maybe it's crazy, but it's my idea and my life. I'm done trying to be what you want me to be." He walked out before Martinson could reply.

* * *

Martinson sat, stunned. He'd come to think of Doug as a pansy—an incompetent wimp who would do whatever it took to keep his lucrative job at M-Gen. Not only had the kid shown he had the balls to walk away, he had also made some valid points regarding the stars and M-Gen's inability to capitalize on their regeneration capability. Doug could easily be replaced as a manager. That wouldn't be a problem, but who would take over management of M-Gen when Martinson retired? Winston was the logical candidate, but he was nearly the same age as Martinson. Would he even want it? This would require some thought.

DEVASTATION

"Queridos," Maria called out, putting on her lab coat.

The greeting lacked its normal cheer. Nana's condition dwelt foremost in her mind, but too many other problems competed for her attention. Working with the stars seemed better than worrying and feeling sorry for herself.

When she turned the corner into the row where the stars were kept, she gasped. The stars' tank was gone!

A feeling of panic crept over her. Was she too late? Had Doug taken them somewhere to perform more experiments on them?

She turned and ran toward Dr. Belleville's office. She had to tell him they were intelligent—get him to help her protect them. What if their mental capability rivaled that of humans?

"Come in," Belleville said when she knocked.

"The stars are gone," she said without preamble.

"Yes. Doug returned to work this morning and requested they be destroyed. Dr. Martinson met with the staff and they concurred. The clones were not acceptable proof of the existence of a new phylum, and the danger the stars represented outweighed their experimental value. I was unable to dissuade them. I'm sorry."

"Destroyed? *Destroyed?* Noooooo …"

* * *

"Miss de la Cruz?"

Maria heard a woman's voice, calm, but insistent. She opened her eyes. Bright lights, a bed with stiff white sheets, a too-clean smell. The infirmary. She recognized the doctor who had taken her blood samples earlier.

Maria struggled to sit up, but the doctor stopped her.

"Let's not rush things. You've had quite a shock."

Then Maria remembered. Everything. The stars, Nana, her arm, Alex. Tears spilled down her cheeks.

"I think it would be best for you to rest the remainder of your shift," the doctor said. "Is there someone who could drive you home?"

Maria strained to make her voice heard. "Alex … uh, Dr. Goodson."

The doctor nodded. "I'll page him. You rest."

As soon as the doctor left, Maria sat up. She found a box of tissues and cleaned her face, finishing just as the doctor returned.

"I'm sorry, Dr. Goodson is gone for the day. Is there someone else?"

Alex gone? But he said he wanted to see me this afternoon. Where could he be?

"A friend, perhaps?"

The question just made things worse. Besides Alex, Janie was the only other friend she had. Would M-Gen even allow her on the property? Who else could she ask?

"If not, we can ask your manager to take you home," the doctor suggested.

Maria's breath caught in her throat. *Dr. Belleville? Dios, no!* She wasn't about to get into a car alone with him.

She looked at the doctor. "May I use the phone?"

The doctor handed it to her. "Thank you." Maria tried to smile but failed. She remembered Janie's vanity number—JanieMc, and punched it in.

Janie answered on the second ring. She sounded happy to hear from Maria even after Maria had asked her to give her a ride home. She was on her way to visit Doug, so she was close by. Maria instructed her to come to the clinic side door.

"The clinic?" Janie repeated. "Is something the matter? Well, of course there is. Dumb question. I'll be there as soon as I can."

"It's not an emergency, Janie. Please drive carefully."

The doctor placed the phone back in its cradle. "I have the results of your blood tests, if you feel like discussing them while we're waiting."

Maria had pushed the problem of her arm to the back of her mind. The loss of the stars took precedence over everything else, even worrying about Nana. She didn't want to talk, but she knew she'd fall apart waiting and doing nothing. She nodded her assent.

"How does your arm feel today?" the doctor asked. "Have you had any fever or nausea?"

"No, why? Is something wrong with my arm? Please don't tell me there's more bad news." Her head fell forward at the prospect.

"No, no," the doctor said, "quite the contrary. Something seems to have triggered an increase in the circulation in your arm. There's no sign of infection or inflammation or any other problem we can identify. All indications suggest it's healthy, growing tissue. That would be consistent with the tingling sensation and the pink color."

"My arm's growing?" Maria's eyes brightened in spite of her emotional load.

"Without a baseline for comparison, I couldn't state that un-equivocally, but yes, I think that's what's happening. It's *possibly* related to your pregnancy, but unlikely."

Maria suddenly felt hot all over, then clammy cold. "My pregnancy?"

"You didn't know?"

Maria felt herself flush. "No," she said, her voice barely audi-ble. She felt a yawning abyss opening beneath her. She had treated the possibility the same as she treated its cause—don't talk about it, don't think about it. Now she had no choice.

The doctor nodded and opened a drawer. "Here's the name of a good OB/GYN," she said, handing Maria a business card. "You should see her at your earliest convenience."

COMMITTED

Maria wanted Alex. Why had he left without telling her? She appreciated Janie's friendship, but longed to curl up in Alex's arms and forget about everything. She thanked the doctor and followed Janie to her car.

"Is your grandmother okay?" Janie asked, once they were on their way.

"Yes. Thank you for asking." The question helped put things into perspective—made her realize how much worse they could be. Nana's welfare was more important to Maria than—*anything*.

"You wouldn't have fainted if it wasn't something serious," Janie observed.

Maria nodded and wiped her cheeks with her palms while she related what had happened to the stars. She didn't mention that their destruction had been Doug's idea. It would only complicate her relationship with Janie.

Janie studied Maria's face a moment. "There's more."

"Yeah." Maria nodded. "While I was waiting for you to come, the doctor dropped a couple of other bombs on me—my arm is growing and I'm pregnant." She gave Janie a disgusted look. "Remind me not to go to *that* doctor again."

"Oh my God." Janie looked at her in disbelief. "I can't believe you can joke about it. I'd be a total wreck."

Maria raised an eyebrow. "You should have seen me earlier."

"Maria, that's wonderful news about your arm. What could have made it start growing?"

"The doctor said it might be related to my pregnancy."

"How do you feel about that news?"

"Wonderful … awful." Maria shrugged and sighed. "I'd given

up long ago ever attracting a man and having a family. Now," she looked out the window without seeing, "I swear I can feel something growing inside of me right this minute, and I'm so excited, I don't know what to do." She shrugged again. "I guess that about sums it up—I have no idea what I'm going to do. Something a lot different than I had planned."

Janie drove the rest of the way home with her hand resting on Maria's.

* * *

Maria's plump neighbor rushed to meet the car.

"Maria, *gracias a Dios* you're home. I've been going crazy with worry. I tried to call you at work, but they said you'd left. Your uncles … they took Nana."

Maria caught her breath. "My uncles? They … where?" she demanded.

"I don't know. They said she'd been declared incompetent. I'm sorry, Maria. They left some papers. Come in. I'll show you." She took Maria by the hand.

Maria followed Yolanda into the house. Janie stayed by the kitchen door, looking around as the other two women talked.

"How was Nana?" Maria asked, her voice suddenly tender. "Did she understand what was happening?"

Yolanda said most of the morning Nana had sat in her room talking to herself—until Maria's uncles came. She became very angry when they told her she had to go somewhere. They wouldn't let her out of their sight, even while she packed her personal things.

"She might have understood what was going on," Yolanda conceded. "When she hugged me goodbye, she told me to tell you to look in the Bible."

Maria shook her head. "I'm afraid that means her mind was in the past again." She turned to Janie. "Nana used to do that when I was younger—tried to get me to find consolation in the Bible."

Maria straightened her shoulders, glancing around the room.

"Yolanda, where are the papers?"

Janie looked at her in amazement. "I can't believe you're taking this so calmly, especially after—"

Maria gave her a quick signal so she wouldn't finish the sentence. Yolanda didn't need to hear the other news. She was a wonderful friend and caregiver for Nana, but she was a terrible gossip.

"I'm okay, Janie. Well, not *okay*," she admitted, "but I've been expecting this. My uncles—" She stopped, closing her eyes for a second. "Long story. I just need to know where they took her so I can get her back."

She took a deep breath. "I'll be all right now. Go see Doug. He'll be wondering where you are."

"You're sure?"

Maria nodded, resolved to do whatever had to be done to get Nana back. She thanked Janie, hugged her, and walked with her to the door.

Janie's car had hardly disappeared down the street when Alex drove in the driveway. He pounded on the kitchen door and entered as soon as he saw Maria coming.

"Maria, are you okay? They said you fainted. I'm so sorry I didn't get back in time to—."

Maria crashed into his arms, cutting him off in mid-sentence.

Alex embraced her, rocking slowly side to side and kissing her forehead. "Who brought you home?" he asked, still holding her.

"Janie."

Alex pushed back from her, holding her shoulders. "Not Janie McLeod!" He looked at her with alarm. "Maria, what if she saw the stars?"

Maria looked at him, puzzled. "She *did* see the stars—when Doug brought her to the lab."

"Not then." He shook his head. "*Now*! If she went into the living room, she'd see 'em."

Suddenly Maria understood why her guppies were in a mixing bowl on the kitchen table. She squealed all the way to the living room.

UNITY

Maria went straight to the aquarium, opened the lid, and plunged her hand into the water.

"Maria, no!" Alex yelled, running toward her. "They'll sting you."

"Don't be silly, Alex. They're my friends. I've been doing this for weeks."

Alex's look of concern turned to one of amazement when Maria caressed Veintidós' skin. Rippling waves of color radiated from the center of the star's faces to the tips of its appendages. No one could misinterpret the meaning of the pattern. The star was purring!

Alex approached the tank. Immediately, Número Uno took up a defensive position between Maria's hand and the front glass where Alex's face appeared. Maria recognized the significance of its flashing pattern. 'Get away. Or else.'

"Número Uno, it's okay," she said. "He's not going to hurt me. He's a good guy. See?" She withdrew her hand from the tank and blotted it on her skirt, then pulled Alex close until both their faces appeared in front of the aquarium, cheeks touching. Alex put his arm around her, cooperating fully.

They watched while Veintidós and Número Uno exchanged patterns—the black-and-white that represented Maria, the orange-and-rust of Alex, and a host of others too fast to distinguish.

Alex looked from the aquarium to Maria and back. "Maria, if I didn't know better, I'd say they were actually talking about us."

Maria smiled. "Well, brace yourself, because very soon you *will* know better. I keep telling you, Alex, they communicate! Once you see Veintidós recite her *a-b-c*'s, you'll realize I haven't been exaggerating."

"*A-b-c*'s?" He yelled. "You can't be serious."

"Oh, yes I can." She said, grinning. "Watch!" She turned to the aquarium. "Veintidós … *A*."

The star pressed one of its faces against the glass, displaying three copies of the letter. The images looked like letters produced by an old dot matrix printer slightly out of alignment.

"*B*," Maria continued.

Three more letters appeared, although not perfectly upright.

Maria opened her mouth to say the next letter, but Veintidós beat her. One by one, she displayed every letter of the alphabet, each in its proper sequence.

Alex looked at Maria, wide-eyed. "They're … ."

He took so long to search for the right words, Maria supplied them for him.

"Sentient?" she asked. "Intelligent? Sapient?" She nodded as she spoke each word.

"I think they have the potential to be all of those. All they need is a teacher." She beamed like a proud parent.

Alex stared at her, open-mouthed. "Maria, this is an incredible discovery! We've gotta report … ."

Suddenly the excitement drained from his face, and his voice trailed off. Maria nodded, knowing he had arrived at the same unhappy conclusion as she. "We can't do a damned thing, can we?" He spread his hands.

Maria shrugged in resignation. The stars were supposed to be dead. If they reported what she'd found, M-Gen would know the stars were still alive … and valuable. They'd take them away from her. Maria couldn't let that happen, even if it meant withholding the discovery.

Alex nodded in agreement. "What a dilemma—the discovery of the century and we don't dare tell anyone."

From the very beginning, Maria had been recording and documenting her sessions with Veintidós in as much detail as she could. M-Gen had excellent recording devices. Someday maybe she would find a safe way to share it. That would relieve some of her guilt about keeping the exciting discovery to herself. She looked at Alex and sighed.

"It's such a relief to finally be able to talk to you about it. I was about to explode."

"I can only imagine. I wish I'd been more supportive." He reached to take her hand.

"Supportive?" she said in astonishment. "Alex, you *saved* them. If it hadn't been for you, they wouldn't be here. How in the world did you get them out of the M-Gen tank?"

Alex had put live brine shrimp in a flask and submerged it in the tank. The ordinary stars just banged up against the sides of the flask, trying to get in. The smart ones figured out to go in through the top.

"What a great idea. When I think how close they came to being destroyed, I start shaking all over. I didn't think you … cared about the stars."

"Maria, you care about the stars. I care about you." He took both of her hands in his.

A lump formed in Maria's throat. "I know you do, Alex. I can't believe I turned you away when you asked me to go out."

She remembered the despair she had felt that afternoon when they named the stars—the futility of forming a relationship that could only hurt them both.

"Are you suggesting the answer might be different this time if I asked again?"

"Yes, you know it would." She slid her hand along his arm, smiling.

"Hm." Alex twisted his mouth to one side for a moment. "What if I ask a different question?" He raised his eyebrows and grinned. "What if I ask you to marry me?"

Maria's eyes flew open and she gasped. "You want to *marry*

me?" The words squeaked from her constricted throat.

Alex's mouth spread into a wide grin. "I do," he said. His arm circled her waist, drawing her body close. He kissed her still-open lips.

"So will you?" he asked, when he finally released her.

"*Dios mío*, yes!" She threw her arms around his neck, almost choking him. "Yes, yes, yes!"

When Maria relaxed her embrace, Alex reached into his jeans pocket. "This is the reason I left work early—the reason I was late gettin' here," he explained, pulling out a box. "I was gonna put the ring in the aquarium with the stars, so you'd find them at the same time. Kinda corny, I guess. This way worked out better." He removed the ring and slid it onto her finger.

* * *

Maria sat on the couch leaning against Alex while she admired her ring. The band was simple, the stone small, but its significance was huge. She was going to be married ... to Alex!

A thought interrupted her celebration. Her smile disappeared. She had said 'yes', but he didn't know she was pregnant. What if ... . She closed her eyes and mouthed a quick prayer.

"Alex, will you still want to marry me if there are two of us?"

"Maria, I've always known you and your Nana'd be a package deal. I'm fine with that."

"I wasn't referring to Nana."

She watched, breathless, as his expression progressed from confusion to wonder, then surprise. His eyes suddenly widened.

"You mean I'm gonna be a *father*?"

A wave of relief washed over her. She let out her breath, grinning as broadly as Alex.

"If you don't mind, I'd like for you to be a husband first," she said. "The sooner, the better."

Alex's mood sobered. "Maria, when were you gonna tell me? I mean what if I hadn't proposed?"

"But you did." She took his hand in hers. "I would have told you. It's your right to know."

"It's also my duty to support a child that I father," he pointed out.

"Yes, it is, but now I know you wanted to marry me without that pressure influencing you. You love me, and I love you, and we'll both love our baby and I'm so happy, I don't know what to do."

* * *

Alex held Maria's diminutive hand. No one but Nana ever touched it affectionately before. The contact felt intimate to her, bordering on erotic. He brought it to his cheek and looked at her curiously.

"Rosemary?"

Maria frowned, the romantic moment ruined. "Alex, that's the second time you've said I smelled like rosemary." She pulled her hand from his and sniffed it. "I don't smell a thing, and furthermore, I don't even like rosemary. I'd never use a product with that fragrance."

"I kinda like it." He picked up her hand again and nuzzled it, then shrugged. "I dunno. Did you wash your hand after touchin' Veintidós?"

Maria blushed. "No, but believe me—you would never mistake her smell for rosemary. Come see for yourself."

She remembered the excitement she felt the first time she'd removed Veintidós from the tank, the fear of getting caught, and the nasty surprise she'd received on bringing the star near her nose.

The two crossed the room to the aquarium. Maria opened the lid and dipped a finger into the tank. "Veintidós?"

The star came without hesitation and wrapped two appendages around Maria's finger. She lifted the animal out of the water, then raised her hand in front of Alex.

"Veintidós , this is Alex. Alex, meet Veintidós."

She let them study one another for a short time, then returned Veintidós to the tank.

Alex wrinkled his nose. "Phew! Guess that answers that. Rosemary—big time."

Maria scowled with confusion. "I don't understand it. I've taken her out of the water many times before. Quite frankly, she stinks … or used to."

She sniffed the air. "This smell is pleasant—somewhat like rosemary I suppose, but very faint. Why is it strong for you and not for me? And why would her odor change?"

"I dunno. The odor apparently stays with you after you handle her. You've prob'ly become accustomed to it so you might not notice it. Maybe it changed because of her injury, or 'cause she's in estrus or something."

"Estrus?" Maria's eyes grew large. "Alex, the smell—not rosemary—the one that night. What if it wasn't man-made? What if the stars released sex pheromones?"

The smell had been all over the lab. It could have affected the other animals, she reasoned, and the two of them got a big dose of it when she opened the lid of the tank.

Alex twisted his mouth sideways. "Sex pheromones only work on members of the same species."

"Are you sure?"

"Well, no, but insects give off pheromones all over the place. We humans could stick our nose down into a jar full of 'em and never smell a thing, much less get turned on. Besides, what survival advantage would result from the stars evolving a pheromone that causes *other* animals to mate?"

"I doubt that it evolved. I suspect it's an anomaly of the cloning process, like their size."

"The chance of that happening has to be almost zero."

Maria wasn't so sure. One could say the same thing about their mental capacity. *That* happened. Alex had seen them demonstrate it. The fact was—someone or something had caused all the animals to mate, including her and Alex. Whether man-made or not, accidental or not, such a substance obviously existed. She preferred to think it came from the stars and not from some pervert at M-Gen who was concocting aphrodisiacs to test on unsuspecting victims—Dr. Belleville?

Alex nodded. "Okay, I prefer that, too, but my money's on the latter. Do you want Belleville to call off the investigation?"

"No. My theory is just that—a theory. If Dr. Belleville can convince us that no one released anything in the lab, that makes it all the more probable that the stars caused the mass mating."

* * *

Maria sighed, half with contentment, half with reluctance. She didn't want to leave her nest within Alex's arms, but she had work to do.

"Alex , maybe Nana has been declared incompetent, but that doesn't mean she can't still live here with me. Do you know a good lawyer ... a cheap one?"

"No, but I'll help you find one. There's no way they can keep her committed when you're willing and able to care for her here."

"I hope you're right, but that'll take time. I want to let her know we're working on the problem. Are you sure we can't give her a message?"

"They said 'no' when I called."

"What if we asked them to give her something? Yolanda said my uncles rushed her when she was packing. Maybe there's something she forgot that we could take to her."

"It's worth a try."

Maria led the way to her grandmother's room. She hesitated at the door, like she'd always done. This was Nana's space. It called for reverence and respect, as did its owner. From Maria's earliest memories, this room had been a sanctuary, a place to come for refuge from bad dreams or bee-stings, a place to hear stories and to play dress-up. More than any other room in the house, this was home. Every detail was etched into her senses—the ticking of the mantel clock, the smell of musty curtains mixed with Nana's perfume, the feel of the wooden bedstead, the massive armoire with its nicks and dents, each with its own story.

She saw the Bible on its stand beside Nana's bed and felt remorse. How hard Nana had tried to make her into a good Catholic. She might have succeeded were it not for the men in the de la Cruz family. Maria had her fill of domineering patriarchs. She didn't need a religion with more of the same.

Maria looked at the bookmark to see what passage Nana had been reading. One of the Psalms. Something else caught her eye. A thick envelope stuck out of the back of the Bible. Maria pulled it out. Her name appeared on the front in Nana's handwriting. She was afraid to open it.

Alex removed the papers, all legal size, and skimmed them. "Your grandmother's name is Elena?"

Maria nodded. She didn't trust her voice.

"Then tomorrow we go get her and bring her home. These papers were drawn up five years ago," he said. "She must have done it right after you turned twenty-one. They appoint you as her legal guardian in the event of her incapacitation."

The news took Maria by surprise. Furthermore, it sounded too good to be true. How could she be Nana's guardian now that someone else had been appointed?

Alex argued that the papers showed what *Nana* wanted to happen. They should take precedence over the appointment her uncles contrived. There was a business card attached to the papers. He volunteered to call the lawyer for her and find out. The lawyer would need to know about Nana anyway.

"I hope he can tell me what to do when my uncles come back," she said. "I have no idea where the deeds are for the property my grandfather owned."

"I'll ask for his advice."

"What a roller coaster ride," Maria said with a sigh. "This has been the worst day of my life, and now it may turn out to be the best one, too. We're going to be married, Nana will come home, my arm, our baby, the stars … ." She slipped her arms around him and laid her head against his chest.

DECISIONS

"Querida!" Maria's grandmother appeared in the doorway of the waiting room accompanied by an elderly volunteer who pushed a metal cart with Nana's belongings.

"Nana," Maria cried, jumping up from her chair. "*Gracias a Dios!*"

Alex and Yolanda stood smiling while the two women embraced, then Maria linked arms with her grandmother and approached Alex. Her face beamed.

"Nana, I would like for you to meet Dr. Alexander David Goodson. Alex, this is my grandmother, Elena Maria Octavia de la Cruz."

Alex stepped forward, taking her hand in both of his. "It's nice to finally meet you."

"The pleasure is mine, Doctor Goodson. Maria does not introduce many gentleman friends to me." She looked at Maria affectionately. "I worry about her sometimes."

Maria moved in beside Alex. "Nana, would this make you worry any less?" She waggled her hand in front of her grandmother, then held it still so she could see the ring.

"Oh, Maria. *Por fin. No se ha muerto Dios de viejo.*"

Alex gave Yolanda a blank look as grandmother embraced granddaughter.

Yolanda smiled. "Literally—God has not died of old age. It means she had almost given up on her prayers being answered. It's an expression from the old country."

Nana hugged Alex just as thoroughly as Maria. His ears flushed pink.

"Querida." Nana took Maria's hand. "I hope you will marry

soon. I don't wish to put pressure on you, but I don't want to be in this place when it happens."

Maria dropped her eyes briefly, then faced her grandmother. "There might be another reason for a quick wedding, Nana."

Nana sighed and shook her head. "I should spank you, but I am too happy to be angry. I want to hold my great-grandchild before my mind is gone."

"Nana, that's not going to happen for a long time."

"Querida, we both know that is not true."

* * *

Nana settled into her rocker, facing the couch, where Maria and Alex sat.

"Are you ready to make some decisions, Maria?" Alex asked.

The question caught her off guard. "What decisions?"

"Like when we're going to get married and where we're going for our honeymoon."

A tingle of excitement spread through Maria's body at the mention of getting married. She still couldn't believe Alex had asked her.

"Nana said 'soon,'" she answered, reaching out to squeeze her grandmother's hand.

"Well, there's a three-day waiting period here in Texas, but we can drive across the Rio Grande right now if you want to."

"Right now?" Maria caught her breath.

"You're the one who said 'as soon as possible,'" Alex reminded her, grinning.

Maria sat frozen in place, hardly able to breathe, much less move, but her grandmother acted for her. Nana rose from her rocker and extended her wrinkled hand.

"Come, Querida. We need to find something appropriate for us to wear."

LANDLORDS

Being married had little effect on Maria's daily schedule. She rose, ate, slept, went to school and work much as she had always done. The big impact was on Alex. He went from sharing a two-bedroom, two-bath apartment with a guy to sharing a two-bedroom, *one*-bath home with two women, both of which had unbending rules about toilet seats and lids. Yolanda helped the transition by keeping Nana at her house in the evening for the first few weeks. Alex liked talking to Nana when she was coherent. When she was not, she sat in the living room absently watching the stars or stayed in her room away from the strange man—*ese hombre desconocido*. Maria wisely let them find their own comfort zone.

She was studying one early afternoon, when she heard car doors slam. She looked out the front window. Three men made their way up the front walk. She opened the door before they knocked.

"*Tíos*, I've been expecting you. Mr. Pinero, attorney-at-law, how fortunate you came, too." She gave him a facetious smile.

Norberto elbowed his way into the living room followed by the other two. They stopped short when Nana walked into the room.

"*Qué diablos!*" Norberto exploded. "What are you doing here? I left explicit instructions—"

"I know about your instructions," Nana spat. "I left some instructions of my own with my lawyer, Sebastian Soto, the last time you lost a legal battle with me."

Norberto's jaw tightened. "We will not lose this one. We have a court order demanding that you turn over the deeds to the property Papá owned."

"Let me see it." She held out her wrinkled hand.

The lawyer pulled a document from his briefcase and handed it to her. She ripped it in half without giving it a glance and shoved the pieces back at Pinero.

"Sebastian has the deeds. Go see him."

Norberto's eyes narrowed. "He'd better have all of them."

"He does." She waited until the men had turned toward the door. "But you don't *get* all of them."

Norberto stopped so abruptly, Gregorio ran into him. Both men turned to face the old woman.

"I put this house in a trust for Maria along with another piece of property the family will give her as a wedding gift."

"Wedding? Pah! She'll never find a—" His ears moved back, and his scalp tightened. "*Which* piece of property?"

"You know which one." Nana held his gaze without blinking.

"*Mierda!* You can't do that. You have no right. Papá wanted to give that—"

"Your father didn't want to give anything to anyone. He was even more selfish than you boys." She waved him away in disgust. "You've got all you need to go home and puff yourselves up as big landowners. Now get out. *Doctor* Goodson, my new grandson-in-law, is coming, and I would be ashamed to introduce you."

Maria said nothing, but held her hand where all could see her rings.

Alex drove in the driveway as the men stormed down the front walk. He hurried in the kitchen door. "Did I miss anything?"

"No ... wait, I take that back. Yes. Nana, what's this about a wedding gift and why was Tío Norberto so angry?"

"Because the land I put in your trust is the only property in the whole lot that produces an income. It has a gold mine on it. It was paying the taxes on all the rest. The boys get to pay them now." She punctuated the statement with a satisfying nod.

I own a gold mine? Maria's eyes lit up. "Nana, I don't mean to sound mercenary, but I'm likely to lose my scholarship sponsors if I can't get anyone to endorse my lab notes. Do you think there's enough money to pay my college expenses?"

"I don't know, Querida. I let Sebastian handle all that. I'm sure he'll be able to tell you." She patted Maria on the arm. "I'm a little tired. I think I'll go lie down a while."

"What a cool grandmother," Alex said when they were alone. "Kinda spunky with a righteous sense of humor. I think I'm gonna like her."

Maria snuggled against him on the couch. "I know. I can't believe how clear-minded she's been since we brought her home. It's almost as if the care home cured her dementia while she was there."

Alex pulled her close. "I know how much that would mean to you."

Maria savored the feel of his arms around her, then sighed. "I guess I should make an appointment to see Mr. Soto. If I've got an income, I need to know how much."

Alex scowled. "Honey, it's not right that your scholarship should suffer because of Doug's stubbornness."

No. It wasn't right, but Maria had learned not to expect 'right' in life. She was a female Hispanic student working at a company dominated by Type A males with Ph.D.'s. She dismissed it with a shrug. She'd been dealing with the problem all her life.

"M-Gen isn't going to stop me. I'll find another sponsor."

"Hmpf, well, you've accused me of being an alpha male before. I'm gonna see what happens on a level playing field."

Maria doubted there was such a place, but welcomed his attempts at chivalry.

NEGOTIATION

"Dr. Goodson," Belleville called out from his swivel chair.

Alex studied the geneticist's face to see if he used the title derisively as Doug did, but the greeting appeared to be genuine.

"Dr. Belleville," Alex answered in kind.

"What brings you to this end of the hall?"

Belleville seldom wasted time on small talk, but his abrupt manner made Alex uncomfortable. "I came to broker a deal," he replied.

"Well, if that briefcase is full of money, you have my attention." Belleville's belly jerked up and down with his laugh.

"Sorry," Alex said. "These are some documents I've gathered in support of Maria's thesis."

In spite of his weight, Belleville pushed himself to his feet quickly and crossed the room to shut the door. "If you've come to persuade me to sign off on her research, you're wasting your time," he said.

"Will you tell me why?"

"Certainly. Several reasons." Although the earlier cordiality disappeared, Belleville remained respectful and seemed willing to answer Alex's question.

Belleville explained that the original specimen had died before anyone outside of M-Gen verified its existence. He said M-Gen's claim to have discovered a new phylum met with considerable skepticism in the scientific world. Endorsing Maria's thesis would have put M-Gen in a very awkward position. First, they would have to confirm they created clones—something Dr. Martinson wanted kept from the media. Second, they'd have to explain why they destroyed them—another unpleasantry. In addition, Maria's thesis depended on a highly controversial premise—her ability to distinguish one star from another. Without it, her observations meant little.

"But she could distinguish them," Alex argued. "I tested her with photographs of the stars. Her accuracy was phenomenal."

"I know. She told me, but be honest, Goodson. A thesis based on a premise validated by using flashcards administered by her husband? If you read that in a scientific journal, what would you think?"

Belleville didn't wait for an answer.

"A thesis at the Master's level is optional. Maria doesn't need one. She's extremely intelligent, very observant, and has excellent grades. She'll graduate at the top of her class without it. Let it go."

"No." Alex glared at the geneticist. "The discovery of a new phylum is a once-in-a-lifetime event. She put her heart and soul into the research and she deserves to receive credit for it."

"It almost sounds like you're threatening me."

"I'd hoped it wouldn't come to that."

Belleville studied Alex over the top of his glasses. "I play poker every Friday night, Goodson. You've got an ace up your sleeve. Let's see it."

Alex revealed his suspicion that the stars were not true clones of the original *Pyramis nana*. Maria had noticed differences, too, but attributed them to the effect mitochondria have on the cloning process or the species used for host cells. It was also suspicious that M-Gen hadn't pursued its claim of having discovered a new phylum. Alex didn't know the details—didn't want to know them, but somehow Belleville and Doug were both involved in the deception.

"How did you arrive at that conclusion?" Belleville demanded.

"When Dr. Martinson asked why the clones seemed so much larger than the original specimen, both you and Doug told him the original specimen was a juvenile. You two agreeing on something—anything—made me suspicious."

"What makes you think it wasn't a juvenile?"

"The recent mass mating episode got me interested in the stars' reproductive systems. Maria wouldn't hear of me cutting open one of the stars, so I dug up the nanography files that we made of the original. I found fully developed *adult* sex organs, not juvenile ones. Once I started looking at the nanograms, I found other inconsistencies which, taken individually, might be over-looked, but taken collectively can't be ignored. The clones are not *Pyramis nana.*"

Belleville leaned back in his chair, rocking and looking at Alex. "You haven't thought this thing through very far, have you, Goodson? You expose me, I get sacked. No one validates Maria's thesis. She loses. M-Gen loses. On the other hand, if you know about the deception and keep mum, that makes you a co-conspirator. There goes your leverage to obtain signatures. Maria loses again."

Alex knew when he came to Belleville's office that his efforts might not be successful. Since Maria couldn't receive recognition for discovering the stars intelligence, he had to try to get her credit for her thesis. He never dreamed his attempt could backfire on him or, worse yet, on Maria. He had to turn this around somehow.

"Dr. Belleville, 'Maria loses' is not an acceptable outcome. M-Gen authorized Maria to write her thesis on the stars, then M-Gen destroyed the stars. It's true, she doesn't need a thesis to get her Master's degree, but she does need it to meet the conditions demanded by her scholarship sponsor. This could end up costing her several thousand dollars and delay the granting of her Master's degree. That's not right."

Belleville didn't respond immediately. His expression was unreadable. Alex promised himself never to play poker with the man.

"I'll take your arguments into consideration, but not now. I have too much on my mind, foremost of which is the mass mating incident and your suspicion it was man made."

"Have you learned anything?" Alex welcomed the change of topic.

"Yes. Besides mine, there were two other cars in the parking lot that night." He stared straight at Alex, and Alex caught his implication. "The next time we meet, I will expect some straight answers from both of you. I am keenly interested in knowing what happened that night."

REGENERATION

"I don't want you to go to work this morning," Maria said, kissing the tip of Alex's nose.

"I don't wanna go, either," he answered, returning the kiss "but I have to, for a few hours at least. Why don't you come, too? H.R. has a bunch of papers we need to fill out, now that we're married."

"Can we tell everyone?" she asked, already preparing to join him.

"Sure. It'll give them something to gossip about," he said, grinning.

"You know, Alex, I don't even care. I'm your wife, I'm pregnant with your child, and I'm happier than I've ever been in my life."

"That makes two of us, for both reasons." He lifted her off her feet in an embrace.

"There's something else, too," she said when he set her down again. Ever since that day in the M-Gen clinic, Maria's excitement had been mounting, and now it had reached the point she could hardly contain it. First because of the possibility, and now the incredible reality.

"Alex, my arm is growing!" she squealed, waving it around in circles. "I wanted to tell you earlier, but I wasn't sure. I am now.

"Look," she said, placing her arm at her side. "My fingertips reach the bottom of my belt. They've never done that before. And see how my arm looks pink and swollen? Well, it's not swollen, it's just bigger, and the pink color is because it's healthy."

"Holy cow, Maria, that's wonderful!" Alex reached to take her small hand in his. "What … ? I mean how … ? I mean … ."

Some of Maria's excitement dissipated when she thought

about revealing her suspicions to Alex. But the coincidences were too strong, the arguments too convincing.

"I think Veintidós is causing my arm to grow," she said. "My arm started growing the same time she began regenerating her appendage, and I've been handling her a lot. Maybe her new appendage produces a substance that rubs off on me. You say I've got the same smell she does now."

Alex looked unhappy. "I, uh, don't wanna throw cold water on your theory, but regeneration doesn't work the way you're thinking. It can't rub off. It's internal—brought about by a release of stem cells."

"What triggers stem cells to be generated?"

"We don't know exactly. I mean there's a gene sequence that codes for some protein to be produced, but we haven't identified the sequence or the protein."

"What if the rosemary smell is the protein?"

"Honey, it's a quantum jump to think a substance the stars produce can trigger regeneration in humans. Our genetic makeup is too dissimilar."

Alex's response disappointed her. If no one had identified what part of the genome codes for regeneration, then how could he argue it wouldn't work in humans?

"Alex, this is too important to dismiss just because it's improbable."

"Well, I agree, but I don't see what we can do about it without getting Belleville involved. The two of us can't conduct the kind of clinical tests that'll be required to prove it works on humans. If you want to discuss it with him, you can bring it up when we go talk to him about the mass mating."

"Oh, God! I forgot about that. Alex, I can't. I can *not* go in there and talk to Dr. Belleville about us having sex. I don't care if we were under the influence of drugs or pheromones or what. I can't. I'll just die of embarrassment!"

CONFESSIONS

"Let's wait in my office 'til it's time for the meeting," Alex suggested, pulling his keys from his pocket and unlocking the door.

"Let's wait here until the meeting's *over*," Maria grumbled, making a face. She entered and plopped down in the guest chair next to his desk. The prospect of talking to Dr. Belleville about what happened that Saturday night made her shudder.

"Honey, I know you're uncomfortable, but I guarantee Belleville's not gonna ask us about havin' sex. He obviously already figured that part out. He'll prob'ly ask us to describe the conditions we observed in the lab prior to the mass mating. We can answer those kinds of questions. Have you decided whether to talk to him about your arm yet?"

"No. I'm convinced Veintidós is making my arm grow, but I'm afraid to talk about it. I'm scared I'll let something slip and he'll find out we have the stars."

Alex shook his head. "We're just not gonna let that happen." He looked at his watch. "It's time."

* * *

"Come in." Belleville nodded Maria and Alex toward chairs near his desk.

She'd barely settled in her seat when he began speaking.

"I will have to leave for a brief meeting in a few minutes. We need to accomplish as much as possible in the time we have. Let's dispense with the administrative issue first, shall we?"

Maria wasn't sure what that meant, but she welcomed the postponement of discussing the *other* issue.

"The decision regarding your lab notes remains the same," he said.

Maria held her chin up and nodded. It was the answer she had expected. Maybe the money from the land Nana gave her … .

"However," Belleville continued, jarring her out of her thoughts, "Dr. Goodson made a valid point. M-Gen authorized you to write your thesis on the stars, then decided to destroy them. You should not be made to suffer because of that decision. I have made arrangements to reimburse your scholarship sponsor. M-Gen will fund your education until you receive your doctorate. Fair enough?"

Maria's mouth dropped open. "Fair? *Dios mío!* It's fantastic! I don't deserve—"

Belleville held up his hand. "I owe you a favor."

Maria looked at Alex, who shrugged, but Belleville continued. "Dr. Martinson is taking early retirement. In the meeting I'll attend shortly, I will be installed as President of M-Gen, thanks to you."

Maria stared at him in astonishment. "Me? Dr. Belleville, I have no idea what you're talking about."

Belleville recounted the sequence of events that had led to his appointment—she and Alex being accused of divulging proprietary information, her revealing that Doug had brought the daughter of Geneering's founder into the aquatics lab. As a result, Doug had been deposed as Dr. Martinson's successor, and Belleville had taken his place.

"But I didn't intend … ."

"I know. Doug's downfall was in no way your fault. It had been building for some time. But your act of telling the truth accelerated the events that put me here. That virtue deserves to be rewarded. Besides, I believe M-Gen will ultimately be the beneficiary of the sponsorship arrangement. End of discussion." He raised his eyebrows. "We have more important things to talk about."

"I … I … May I … have a moment with Alex?" Maria stammered.

Belleville scowled and looked at his watch. "Very well—a moment," he emphasized.

The minute they were out in the hall, Maria threw her arms around Alex. "My doctorate!" she squealed. "I can't believe it."

Alex pressed his lips together. "Yeah, me either."

Maria heard the doubt in his voice. "What?" she asked, pulling back to look at him. "You don't think he'll follow through?"

"I don't know what to think, Maria. If you're not right about the stars—if their pheromones didn't cause the mass mating, then he or someone else did. He could turn this gift of M-Gen's sponsorship into a bargaining chip. Let's see what develops."

Belleville sat waiting as Maria and Alex took their seats. He made a teepee with his fingers against his lips.

"The mass mating."

Maria inhaled audibly. Belleville nodded and faced her.

"Maria, I am a very private person. Dr. Goodson will confirm that it is difficult enough for me to share my scientific knowledge, let alone divulge personal information. I'm truly sorry for placing you in this awkward situation, but I must … I *must* … have answers to my questions."

Maria gripped Alex's arm, but Belleville continued speaking.

"Dr. Goodson was correct to suspect that some of my colleagues are engaged in unauthorized research. Be that as it may, no one, including me, is involved in producing substances which even remotely could have caused the mass mating. The agent was not man-made. We are sufficiently familiar with all the other animals in the lab. They didn't cause it. By elimination, that leaves the stars. Fantastic as it may seem, I believe the stars caused the mass mating."

Belleville peered over his glasses at the two of them.

"If, as I suspect, the stars released mating pheromones—pheromones whose influence extended to humans, then I can't begin to impress on you the importance of the discovery to mankind."

Maria steeled herself, preparing to answer his questions, but Alex touched her arm.

"Why so important?" he asked. "It seems to me it's only a matter of academic interest now that the stars are gone."

Belleville looked first at Alex, then Maria, his expression deadpan. "The stars are not gone."

Maria caught her breath. A feeling of panic invaded her. *He knows we have the stars!*

A scowl replaced the poker face.

"I refuse to allow the only members of a heretofore unknown phylum to be destroyed because of Doug's warped sense of justice. Maria," he looked at her with compassion, "I sincerely apologize for the emotional turmoil I caused you, but I could not reveal my actions at the time. I took the first star Doug cut plus two others to my own home. The remaining clones are preserved in cryogenic storage. They can be revived whenever circumstances permit."

Maria's eyes flew open. "You took ... you preserved—?" She interrupted herself, fearful that she would let something slip in her excitement. Relief flooded over her. *He doesn't know!*

Belleville had spent months mapping the genome of the stars, comparing the one Doug cut with ones with no injuries. He believed he had identified the genetic sequence that controls the stars' regeneration! Even though he had located the same sequence in the human genome, he seriously doubted it would be possible find a trigger to activate it in humans. When he heard about the mass mating, deduced that the stars caused it, and realized their pheromones possibly *did* affect humans, he redoubled his efforts to find the protein that induces regeneration in the stars. Perhaps it could be made to trigger regeneration in humans.

"Now that Dr. Martinson is stepping down, I am prepared to bring to bear all of M-Gen's resources to discover the substance that activates regeneration if there is any chance it can be used to benefit humans. This has been the goal of my entire career and I sense that you have knowledge that is critical to the achievement of that goal."

Tension in the room was so palpable, Maria let out a yelp when Belleville's phone rang.

He scowled at the interruption. "Yes?" he snapped. "Oh … I … very well. I'll be there shortly."

He pinned Maria and Alex to their chairs with the intensity of his gaze. "This meeting is not over. You will remain here until I return, be that a minute or an hour. Understood?"

ROSEMARY

Alex looked at Maria in astonishment. "Holy cow, Maria. I learned more about Belleville in the last five minutes than in the past five years of working with him."

"I know! Besides being generous—and I don't think that's a trick—he's considerate of my feelings and obviously cares about the stars. He saved them!" Her voice squeaked with excitement.

"Yeah, he and I must have just barely missed each other!"

"And Alex, he's concluded that the stars *did* cause the mass mating. That means their pheromones do affect humans."

"True, but we still don't have any conclusive evidence that Veintidós is causing your arm to grow."

"My arm is evidence. It's just not proof."

Maria felt certain what caused the rosemary smell was the substance that Dr. Belleville was looking for. Veintidós didn't acquire the smell until she started regenerating, and Maria didn't get it until her arm started growing *after* she'd been handling the star. That was too much of a coincidence to ignore.

"Wait a minute, Maria. I just thought of something. The smell can't be it. Nana has the smell. I noticed it when she hugged me at the care home. *She's* never touched Veintidós."

Maria looked up in surprise. "Nana has the smell? You never mentioned that."

"No. You weren't too happy when I told you *you* smelled like rosemary. I figured I'd better keep my mouth shut about Nana."

She gave him a reproachful look. "Alex, I'm not going to get angry with you for telling the truth." She paused, pursing her lips. That did throw her theory into doubt, though. Nana had never been near the stars. Not until she came back from the care home, at least.

"I don't know, Maria. There's somethin' going on here that we're missing. I agree about the coincidences, but if Nana's got it, she didn't get it from the stars."

Maria grabbed his arm. "Alex! What if *I'm* contagious? I've certainly touched Nana. She could have gotten it from *me*."

Alex scowled. "Why would Nana get it and not me? I don't have the smell. Besides, she and I don't have any missing limbs. What would we be regenerating?"

Suddenly Maria's eyes grew wide. "*Santo Dios*! Her mind! What if that's what is regenerating—the cells that have died in her brain?"

Nana's coherency had been improving ever since they brought her home. Her lucid periods hadn't lasted that long in months. Maria trembled with emotion. Nana's mind whole again? Could it be possible?

Alex stared at her. "Wow. I mean holy cow! I mean—"

Maria sucked in her breath. "Oh, *Dios mío!* What if it's only Veintidós that produces the substance? If Dr. Belleville finds out we have the stars, he'll take them away from us. As soon as Veintidós' appendage heals, he'll chop off another just to keep her producing the substance. I can't let that happen!"

"No. We're gonna hafta find a better place to hide 'em. Anyone who comes into the house can see 'em, and Nana or Yolanda could say the wrong thing to someone."

Maria closed her eyes. "There's only one way to make sure they're safe … free them." Her voice quivered.

"You mean like put 'em in the Rio Grande?"

"No, of course not. They're tropical." Maria frowned, thinking. "The only logical place is Peru—where they came from."

"Jeez, Maria, how're we gonna do that? And do you want to? What if Veintidós is making your arm grow and Nana's mind heal? You free the stars and then find out the effect fades—you need con-

tinuous exposure to keep the regeneration going. Are you willing'
to sacrifice your arm and your grandmother's mind for the sake of
the stars' freedom?"

Maria thought a long moment before answering. She would
love to have two good arms, shake hands like everyone else, and
walk into a room of strangers without receiving stares, but those
were luxuries. She could live without them—had for more than
twenty years. Nana's situation was different. It tore Maria apart to
watch Nana's mind deteriorate. If she were sure Nana would get
her mind back, she'd be sorely tempted to keep the stars. That was
the problem. She *wasn't* sure. What if she denied them their freedom, so her arm would grow and Nana's mind improve, only to
find out the stars had nothing to do with it? How selfish!

"Alex, the stars are intelligent creatures. Just how intelligent I
don't know yet, but it doesn't make any difference. Intelligent beings should have control over their own destiny. I have no right to
keep them captive in an aquarium when there's a whole world out
there for them to explore."

"What about the world you're exploring—communicating
with Veintidós. Can you just walk away from that—cold turkey?"

Maria looked at the floor. "I didn't say it would be easy."

Alex pursed his lips and nodded. "I support whatever decision you make."

Maria took his hand in hers. "My decision is to free them—
somehow."

DEAL

Belleville lumbered back into the office, wheezing from his walk. "Now where were we?" he asked when he turned his chair to face them.

Maria remembered very well where they were and wished they weren't.

"Are congratulations in order?" she asked.

"What? Oh … yes, I suppose. Thank you, but don't try to distract me. Are you ready to answer my questions?"

"Not exactly," she said, forcing herself to face him. "I … we … will confirm that the stars' mating pheromones affect humans," she felt herself redden, "but I see no need to elaborate on that topic. It's the mechanism that activates regeneration you're interested in."

"Absolutely, but the search for that mechanism could take years and cost millions. Any information you can give us about the pheromones affect on humans may accelerate the process significantly."

Maria looked a question at Alex, half hoping he would stop her. Revealing what she knew—*believed*—could have a huge impact on her life and the lives of everyone she loved, including the stars. Millions could be made whole again, eliminating their suffering and restoring normality to their lives.

Alex squeezed her hand. "Your call," he said, leaving the decision to her.

Maria nodded. It *was* up to her. She took a deep breath. "Dr. Belleville, if I can enable you to bypass that long and costly search, will you make a deal with me?"

Belleville jerked back as if he'd been slapped. "Are you suggesting you know what activates it?" He looked at her in astonishment. "The mechanism that activates regeneration? Impossible! You're a student—an intelligent one, I'll grant you, but still only a student. There's no way you could have identified it."

Suddenly his expression became hard. "And what is this deal? Maria, I am surprised and dismayed to learn that you, of all people, would hold such knowledge hostage for your own personal interests."

"Not *my* interests—the *stars*. I want to make sure they'll be safe."

"Oh." The suspicion disappeared from his face. "I concur. By all means. A resource that valuable? Rest assured M-Gen will keep them under the tightest security available. They'll be safe."

Maria looked at him with a raised eyebrow. "Not from M-Gen."

She remembered all too well the things Doug had done, with or without M-Gen's sanction. So long as the stars were at M-Gen, they were vulnerable.

Belleville sat up straight, wary again. "And how exactly would you propose we provide for their safety?"

"I want you to agree to revive the ones that are frozen and arrange for all stars, including the ones you have in your home, to be transported to Peru, where Alex and I will personally supervise their release."

"Release? Don't be ridiculous. Without the stars we'd have no hope of finding the activation mechanism. So that's what this is all about? Freeing the stars?"

His tone softened. "Maria, I realized when you fainted how fond you had become of the stars, and I apologize again for the anguish I caused you. But I must point out that you are doing the same thing to me—giving me hope that you've discovered the secret to regeneration, only to find out it's a ploy to free the stars. Please, no more tricks."

"Dr. Belleville, I give you my word this isn't a trick."

His eyes opened wide. "You mean … ?"

Maria nodded. "I mean I believe I've discovered the mechanism—a substance, actually—that activates regeneration, not only in the stars, but in humans as well. I have no proof; we'll have to conduct tests. If I'm wrong, I'll cry as hard as you. In any case, I won't ask you to release the stars until we both agree that we have successfully activated regeneration in humans and can continue to do so without the stars. Fair enough?"

"Oh my, oh my, oh my! And you thought *you* could negotiate," Belleville said to Alex. "Done!" he shouted and rose to shake Maria's hand. He didn't even hesitate when she offered her right one. "Now what is this substance, and when can I have it?"

Maria looked at Alex and then back to Belleville, smiling. "I just gave you a sample. Smell your hand."

His frown became a look of puzzlement. "Why that's rosemary! My mum used to put it in her steak and kidney pie. I don't understand. What's rosemary got to do with—?"

Maria waved her hand to interrupt him. "Maybe you should sit down," she suggested.

He did so, but drew his chair forward, giving her his full attention. This was it—the point of no return. Strangely enough, an aura of calm settled over her as she began to share the miracle of her discovery.

"My arm is growing," she said, "regenerating, if you will. Two inches so far. It started right after I handled the star Doug cut. Before it was injured, the star smelled quite unpleasant—*stunk*, actually. When it began regenerating its appendage, it began giving off the rosemary smell."

"That's odd," Belleville interrupted. "I have the other star Doug cut. I agree, it stinks, but it doesn't smell any differently than the uninjured one. Are you certain the smell was coming from the star?"

"Yes, I'm certain. That star was one of my favorites—one that I was in the habit of touching and handling without gloves. I believe the substance was transferred to me by way of that contact. Now *I* smell like rosemary."

Belleville smelled his own hand. "Yes, it's quite pungent. But, Maria, don't you see—we can't release the stars. We need them to produce the regeneration agent."

"No. That's why I asked you to sit down." Maria had to force her voice around the lump in her throat. "I believe my grandmother's mind is regenerating. She's suffered from dementia for years, until recently, when she, too, started smelling like rosemary. She couldn't have gotten it from the stars. She's never been near them. She could only have gotten it from me. I don't just have the *smell*, I am producing the *substance*!"

"Good Lord, do you have any idea what that means?"

Maria closed her eyes and nodded. "It means that with as simple a gesture as a hug, a kiss, or a loving touch, one human being can give another the blessed gift of being whole again—all thanks to the stars."

* * *

Belleville sat his chair, stunned, yet his eyes shone bright with excitement. "If this pans out, I may have to get D.J. to come back. I'll be too busy to manage M-Gen."

He remained quiet for a moment, then looked up. "Dr. Goodson, would you go to the lab and bring back a culture tube—55 milliliter?"

Alex looked at Maria, who shrugged.

When Alex returned, Belleville handed Maria a packet of alcohol pads. "If you will, please swab the skin of your hand, particularly your palm and in between your fingers, and place the pad in this tube. The alcohol will leave your skin dry, but I have hand lotion in my desk."

Maria did as instructed and Belleville capped the tube. The smell of alcohol hung in the still air of his office.

"Maria, if this substance is what you suspect it is, then I can't stress enough the importance of you minimizing contact with other people. Imagine what could happen if you inadvertently trigger regeneration in someone with an artificial limb or organ without them first having the prosthesis removed. Someone like me?"

"*Dios mío!* Dr. Belleville. Omigod! I … are you … do you … ?"

"No, but I'm disappointed that as a scientist, you didn't think about that. The three of us are going to be working together as a team, and we must carefully consider every move we make to avoid mistakes of that sort.

"As soon as I can obtain the animals, I'll need you to expose one group of them to the substance and another group to your presence, but without contact, to determine if the mechanism is airborne. I'll start tests immediately, but we will not have conclusive results for several weeks. Meanwhile, if I had the authority and a facility, I would have you sealed in a plastic bubble and locked in a guarded tower." He peered over the top of his glasses at her.

"There are people who will go to any lengths—*any* lengths—to get their hands on this substance or you or the stars. And you can imagine what the prosthetics industry will do if they get wind of the discovery. You be *very* careful."

Maria and Alex slipped out of the office, leaving Belleville gazing at the tube. The tiny sample it contained could touch the lives of almost every person on the planet.

When they reached the hall, Alex grinned. "He looked like a kid who just got a brand new X-box."

"Yes." Maria smiled, too. "I share the feeling. I'm going to be having as much fun as he is—maybe more."

"The stars?"

"You *bet*, the stars. Alex, Veintidós learned the alphabet after only seven repetitions—in less than an hour. That's phenomenal! That's better than the most precocious human child can do. Letters are total abstractions to the stars, yet they not only remember them, they remember them in their proper sequence. That's exactly what words are."

"You mean you're gonna teach 'em to *read*?"

"You'd better believe I'm going to *try*. I've been thinking about it ever since Veintidós displayed her first letter. Now that I'm convinced they have the capacity, I'm going to help them develop it."

JAKE

GENEERING, EXECUTIVE ROW:

"Hi, Daddy."

Janie gave Jake a daughterly peck on the cheek, wrinkling her nose at the smell of stale cigar smoke that permeated his clothes. She started to sit in a leather chair near his desk, but hesitated. The jutting tusks of a warthog mounted on the wall above the chair gave her the shivers. This was a man's room, with dark wood paneling, massive furniture, and dead animals hanging on the walls. There weren't many safe places to sit. She chose a chair as far from the menagerie as possible.

Jake had tried to make Janie into the son he never had. He succeeded in engendering in her a love for the out-of-doors, but the more she learned about guns and what they did, the less she liked them. Instead of specializing in zoology, she chose botany. Not many people killed plants for trophies.

Jake punched STOP on the player and removed his headphones. "You might want to hear this."

"If that's from M-Gen, I'm not interested," she said. "I came to visit, not play spy." Janie dutifully visited her father on a regular basis, and if she learned something useful to Geneering, she would pass it on to him, but she would not participate in his nefarious activities.

"Would you be interested if you thought there was a chance your boyfriend's hand could grow back?"

Janie stared at him. "Daddy, are you serious? Is that possible?"

She closed her eyes, imagining what that could mean for her waning relationship with Doug. Loss of his hand had had a huge impact on their lovemaking.

"I don't *know*," he grumbled. "I didn't think so, until I heard this tape. Now I'm not sure. Here … you listen and tell me what you think." He unplugged the headphones to activate the speaker and pressed PLAY.

" *… Have you decided whether to talk to him about your arm yet?"*

"No. I'm convinced Veintidós is making my arm grow, but I'm afraid to talk about it. I'm scared I'll let something slip and he'll find out we have the stars."

Janie's hand flew to her mouth. "Oh, my God! That's Maria."

"You *know* this person?" Jake stared at her in astonishment.

"I … we … yes, I met her when Doug took me to M-Gen to see the clones."

Janie was so stunned at what she'd heard, she could hardly think. If something could cause Maria's arm to grow, could it work for Doug? Jake didn't give her time to reflect.

"What the hell does she mean when she says something or other is making her arm grow?" he asked.

"I think … at least she *could* mean exactly what she said. She has a stunted arm. She told me it was growing."

Jake stared at her. "You know someone working at M-Gen who told you her stunted arm is growing? And you were going to tell me this *when*?"

"Daddy, I swear had no idea she meant *regenerating*. You know I would have told you."

Jake frowned, then nodded. "Yeah, I guess you would. Alright, then, next question—what the hell is *bainty dose*? It's not in any pharmaceutical database."

"It's not a drug. It's a number. Veintidós is Spanish for twenty-two. Could it be a batch or sample number used in a test?"

"Sure, but why would she say it in Spanish? He scowled, mumbling to himself. "Twenty-two. Twenty-two. Why does that ring a bell?" Suddenly he slapped his forehead. "Wait, wait wait. What's her last name?"

"De la Cruz."

"That's it!" Jake snapped his fingers. "It was hers—the note-book we got from M-Gen."

He spun around in his chair and opened a nearby filing cabinet, digging until he found the folder of reproduced pages. He skimmed to the part he was looking for.

"Yes!" He jabbed a finger into the notebook. "Number one, number thirteen and number twenty-two—the three clones she claimed she could tell apart. And number twenty-two is making her arm grow."

He smiled hungrily. "We've got to get some of those clones!"

Janie shook her head "It's too late. They've been destroyed. Doug convinced his dad they were too dangerous to keep around."

"*What?* Of all the stupid … wait a minute." Jake waved his hand. "She said *is* making—present tense. And she's scared Belleville will find out she has the stars—present tense again. You know what?" He smiled slyly. "I think they're *not* dead. I think she squirreled them away someplace."

"She couldn't have. She was so upset, she fainted when she heard they'd been destroyed. She called me to drive her home from the M-Gen clinic."

"Okay, then somebody else rescued the clones—at least number twenty-two. Do you know who the guy was on the tape?"

"I would assume Dr. Goodson. Doug said he was involved with the clones."

It surprised Janie how easily she gave her father the information. She knew him well enough to know how little he valued someone else's privacy.

Jake drummed his fingers on the desk. "Okay, so here's what we know. Her stunted arm is growing. Clone number twenty-two is making it happen. Most likely Goodson has it stashed somewhere. And Belleville doesn't know."

Jake pursed his lips and stared off into space. "An animal that can induce regeneration in humans. Wow! If I can find number twenty-two before Belleville does—before he even *learns* about it, I could scoop M-Gen for millions. Billions!"

"What are you going to do?"

Janie didn't like the way Jake's eyes lit up. It was pretty obvious money, not compassion motivated him ... and she was helping him.

"I'm going to look for the clone," he said. "Maybe the rest of these tapes will give me a clue, but my information sources are drying up."

As soon as he became president, Belleville had replaced M-Gen's custodial company, and Jake lost his moles there. With no one to collect the memory cards or replace the batteries, the bugs would become useless.

"If he switches security contractors, I'll be up shit creek."

Janie pouted her lip. "Poor you."

"Hey, give me a break," he carped. "If it wasn't for my bugs at M-Gen, you wouldn't have known Doug was going back to Peru. Which reminds me—did Doug ever mention why D.J. fired his secretary?"

"He said it was for divulging proprietary information."

Jake laughed when he heard her say that. "Oh, that's rich."

"Well, didn't she? You told me you learned about M-Gen's expeditions to Peru from her."

"Not from *her*—from the *bug* at her desk."

"You mean she wasn't one of your plants?"

"No. That's what's so funny. She was probably the best employee Martinson had."

The information disturbed Janie—not only because she'd been tricked into causing the woman's dismissal, but because of her father's obvious indifference.

"Daddy, you should be ashamed of yourself. A woman's career has been ruined and her reputation sullied and you're gloating about it." She gave him an accusing look. "I love you, but sometimes you make it damned difficult to like you."

He dismissed her criticism with a shrug. "You like me well enough when my information is useful to *you*."

He returned Maria's notebook to the filing cabinet. "Thanks for the help. I'll keep you posted."

* * *

Janie drove paying little attention to traffic. Her thoughts were occupied by one question—would it work for Doug? She openly admitted that sex was a big part of her relationship with Doug, and he had been skilled with his hands. To what ends would she go to help him get his hand back?

To what ends would her *father* go? That worried her even more. His undisguised greed and his ruthless motives and methods scared her, yet she'd been all too willing to help him. She could even have put Maria in danger if Jake thought she had the clones.

"Oh my God!" she said out loud.

She does *have the clones! They're in her aquarium. That's why the guppies were in a mixing bowl on the table. Alex must have put them there before I brought Maria home.*

Now *what do I do?*

SEVERED

"Hi, Honey." Alex greeted Maria as she entered the aquatics lab from the parking lot. "You're here early. What's up?" He gave her a quick kiss.

"Alex, you'll never believe it," she squealed. "In fact, you *still* won't after you see it."

"See what?" he asked.

Maria pulled her data pad from her purse. "Watch," she said as she called up a video clip. "The letters come pretty fast, and they don't scroll—they sort of flash, so pay attention."

Alex's eyes opened wide as he watched Veintidós rapidly display block letters spelling Maria's name followed with the familiar black-and-white pattern that the stars had always used to represent Maria.

"Holy cow, Maria. I mean *holy cow!* You said you were gonna, but I didn't really think you could—didn't think *they* could. How'd you do it—teach her?"

Maria beamed. "It was actually fairly easy. I showed her my picture, spelled my name with the flash cards, then pronounced it. It only took five repetitions for her to grasp that the sounds and the letters represented the picture and me. I taught her her own name, yours, and the other two stars', too." Maria grabbed Alex's arm. "Alex, I'm going to be able to *talk* to her!" She held his hand and danced around him.

"Wow, Maria. And I thought *my* news was exciting."

"What?" She inhaled abruptly. "Dr. Belleville has test results? Already?"

"Yup." He smiled at her. "The mouse, the pig, and the chimp—they've *all* started regenerating."

"Alex. If it works on three other species of mammal, it *has* to be what's happening to me."

"That must've been what Belleville thought, too. He's sporting a bandage on his left pinky."

Maria gasped. "*Dios en el cielo!* Dr. Belleville severed his own finger?"

Alex grinned and nodded. "The tip anyway."

Belleville had claimed it was an accident, but Alex said he figured Belleville did it so no one else would learn about the tests. That would be one way to keep it tight.

"The guy's got guts."

"I can't believe he did that!" Maria exclaimed. "*I* certainly wouldn't, and I'm convinced it works."

"He must be, too. He told me to start thawing out the stars he put in cryogenic storage. As soon as his finger starts growing, we can take them to Peru."

"Now? But I … ." Her voice trailed off.

For weeks—*months* now—Maria had been plotting and planning to free the stars, determined to overcome all obstacles blocking their release. With the last hurdle cleared, it was as if she had been pushing hard against a door and someone suddenly jerked it open, causing her to lose her balance. Now what?

"Yeah, I was wonderin' if you'd still want to release them after what you just discovered. Y' know, Belleville was right. M-Gen can provide the best security available. Even if he's convinced we don't need the stars to induce regeneration in humans, I'm sure he'll still agree to protect them. I think it'd even be safe to reveal what you've learned about their intelligence. We could bring the stars back to the aquatics lab and you could continue to work with them here."

"Alex, I don't know what to do. I don't disagree with anything you just said, but the more I recognize how intelligent they are, the more imperative it becomes to free them. Intelligent beings should have control over their own destinies. I have no right to keep them captive in a ten-gallon aquarium when there's a whole world out there for them to explore."

"I … uh … don't wanna complicate things, but I wonder if you've considered the ethics from another viewpoint. You agree that their intelligence is likely an anomaly of the cloning process. That means that instead of returning the stars to an environment where they've existed in harmony for millennia, we could be unleashing a man-made, intelligent species onto an unsuspecting planet."

Maria thought for a moment, frowning all the while. Alex might be right, but she thought he was being overly dramatic about it. "What could three intelligent creatures that size do to endanger the planet, as you put it?" she asked.

"Reproduce."

Maria shook her head. "I don't think they can. I started looking for signs as soon as I learned I was pregnant."

All of the stars had mated—every one of them, but Maria had seen no eggs, nor young, nor swelling of their bodies indicating they were carrying them. She suspected they were sterile, but even if they weren't, she thought they would have as much difficulty producing viable offspring as Dr. Belleville had producing viable clones. He had started with several hundred clones. Less than seven percent lived long enough to transfer to the aquatics lab. Of those, another eight died within the first month. Maria didn't know how much longer *any* of them would live.

"What about the work you're doin' with Veintidós? Honey, you're communicating with another creature whose intelligence could possibly equal *ours*. Can you just walk away from that? Can you turn them loose without telling anyone that there are *two* intelligent species on this planet?"

Maria looked at the floor. The thought of never talking to Veintidós again brought tears to her eyes, but the ethical question was equally agonizing. The stars had the right to control their own destiny. She was sure of that, but did the rest of the world have the right to know about them? To interact with them? What if the *stars* didn't want that?

"Ahhh," she wailed, putting her interlocked hands on her head and trying to pull her head into its shell. "I don't know, I don't know, I don't know!"

"Alright, Honey." Alex squeezed her hand. "You don't have to decide just yet. I have an idea that might at least make things easier. What if we bring your three stars back to M-Gen and mix 'em in with the ones I revive from cryogenic storage? Nobody but us would know the difference. You could continue working with Veintidós and decide later whether to free them or reveal their intelligence."

HEIST

JAKE BLUMENTHAL'S OFFICE:
"How well do you know this Maria?" Jake asked.

Janie fidgeted in her chair near his desk. She liked Maria—liked having a friend the same age with similar education and common interests. Jake's interest in Maria bothered her. She tried to think how to answer without encouraging him.

"Not well," she said. "We've met in person a few times and traded e-mails. Why?"

"Because I may need you to pick her brain. Goodson moved out of his apartment. If they're coworkers, she may know where he lives. I need to know so I can find the clones."

"Daddy, I'm worried what you're going to do."

"I'm going to find the damned clones—*steal* them, if you want me to be explicit."

"I know that. It's how you do it that worries me."

"There's no reason for you to worry. *You're* the one who'll be asking her questions." He tilted his head and looked at her suspiciously. "You know something, don't you?"

His eyes narrowed. "Dammit, Janie, this is too important for you to start getting squeamish on me. You want my help, you've got to help me. Do you want your man to get his hand back or not?"

Janie had already made that decision, but each step toward that goal took her deeper into her discomfort zone. She closed her eyes briefly.

"They just got married," she told him. "Maria said he was going to move to her place. I think the clones may be there."

Jake glared at her across the desk. "Thank you," he growled. "Now where does she live?"

"I don't know the address. I think I remember how to get there."

"Alright, then. Show me." Jake pushed back from his desk.

"What are you going to do?"

"Stop asking that question! Show me where she lives. I'll send someone to check if the clones are there. If she's got them, I'm going to take them.

"Not *me* … not *now*," he said in response to her reaction. He stood up. "Come on. Let's go."

* * *

AQUATICS LAB:

"Look, Alex." Maria smiled as she turned her data pad for him to see.

The clip showed Maria's finger stroking Veintidós, then a sequence of letters appearing on the star's skin: MARIA TOUCH #22.

"Her first sentence!" Maria threw her arms around Alex, hugging him in her excitement. "She knows 'touch', 'come', and 'go', and she learned 'tank' and 'hand' and 'net' today."

"Amazing," Alex said. "How're you doin' it?"

"It's easy and *fun*!" Maria grinned.

She had begun by showing Veintidós cards with letters on them and saying the name of the letter. It was an easy step to show flash cards with short words and pronounce them. Later she added pictures to the cards. By speaking and showing a picture with the word, she associated each concept with multiple senses, reinforcing the learning process. Veintidós understood several spoken words, plus she could respond by displaying letters and patterns on her skin.

"Do you think she can actually read?"

"Why not? We humans learned 'See Spot Run' by hearing someone read the words while we looked at them and the pictures. I'm working on a comic strip showing them going from the M-Gen aquarium into the flask you used, then being in my home aquarium. If I add another panel on that same strip showing the stars without a container, maybe Veintidós will get the concept of 'no limits' or 'free'. I hope so. Abstract concepts are the most difficult to communicate."

"I wish I was havin' as much luck reviving the stars in cryogenic storage."

"Trouble?"

"Yeah. They're not surviving the thaw."

Alex had even asked Belleville for help, but he said Alex was doing everything he would do. If he couldn't solve the problem and get some other stars in the tank, they wouldn't be able to hide Maria's three.

"I'm sorry to hear that," Maria said. "I mean there's no emergency, but I *would* like to move them to M-Gen soon. I'm spending so much time with Veintidós, I'm letting other things slide. If she were here at M-Gen, then I could work with her during my shift."

"I'll keep trying. I guess we could bring your three back and I could claim they were ones I revived."

"Let me see if I can develop a better vocabulary with Veintidós. I'd like to be able to tell her what we're going to do—at least let her know they'll be moving again."

* * *

JAKE BLUMENTHAL'S OFFICE:

"Wants him *back*?" Jake yelled. "What the hell for?"

"According to Doug, Belleville wants to concentrate on some new project. He wants Dr. Martinson back so he doesn't have to manage M-Gen at the same time," Janie explained.

"The son-of-a-bitch learned about her arm regenerating. That's the new project. Dammit to hell and back! I was hoping he wouldn't find out. I need to move fast while the clones are still at her place. You said Goodson works nine to five and the girl works four to midnight, right? That leaves nobody home but the old lady from … say three-thirty to well after five. Plenty of time. I'll send some guys tomorrow."

"Daddy, please … ."

"I know, I know—don't hurt anyone. C'mon, Janie. They'll be armed with a dip net and a bucket for chrissake."

* * *

Maria sat on a piano bench in front of her aquarium. Rays of sunlight peeked through the drapes, illuminating motes of dust that floated in the still air.

"Light, dark … Veintidós go to tank with rock." Maria spoke and flashed the words followed by a picture of the stars' original tank at M-Gen. "Veintidós and Trece and Número Uno go to tank with rock."

¿LIGHT DARK?

"Yes, tomorrow," Maria confirmed.

She was pleased to see the star using the Spanish upside-down question mark at the beginning of the query. It had taken three days for Veintidós to grasp the concept of questions. Maria smiled to herself, more than eager to deal with the onslaught of *why*'s she knew would come, if she could only figure out how to demonstrate interrogatives.

She noticed Veintidós and Trece exchanging patterns, then Veintidós turned to face Maria. "#13 FEAR TANK WITH ROCK"

"Trece's afraid? Why?" Maria asked, immediately realizing *why* was not in their vocabulary. "Veintidós teach Maria."

"NET COME. STAR GO. HAND COME. #22 HURT. #13 FEAR HAND. #13 EAT HAND"

"Trece remembers Doug cutting you and the other star? No! Trece, please don't be afraid. That's not going to happen again. Oh!" Maria let out a plaintive cry as she scrambled to assemble her flash cards.

"Not fear. Net not come. Hand not come. Maria with Veintidós and Trece and Número Uno."

"*Ay, Dios!*" she wailed. "Humanity's first contact with another intelligent species and *that's* the impression we made! Queridos, I promise you you're going to have control over your own lives just as soon as I can make it happen."

* * *

A beige Buick LaCrosse cruised slowly down the street. The two occupants looked at Maria's house as they drove by. Her car was gone. They made a U-turn at the end of the block and pulled to the curb in front of the house. A dog challenged the unusual activity. Someone yelled, and the dog issued a final halfhearted warning. The neat, conservatively-dressed young couple got out of the car and walked to the front door. The man held a book and some pamphlets in his hand, the woman, a large purse. He rang the bell. A moment later he rang it again.

The man moved between the woman and the door, donning gloves and unfolding a set of tools from his pocket. He had the lock open in seconds. They stepped in, closing the door behind them. He pointed and she moved quietly down the hall, checking each room as she passed by. She returned, shaking her head. No one was home.

In the living room, darkened with drapes against the harsh Texas sun, the man found the aquarium. He slid the tank forward on the table until he could get his fingers under the edges. Grunting with the effort, he lumbered with it into the kitchen. The woman removed a net and plastic bowl from her purse and held the net over the sink. Her partner upended the aquarium, slopping water onto the countertop and floor, but managing to pour most of the water through the net. The woman dumped the wiggling contents of the net and a small amount of water into the bowl and snapped the lid on it.

"Let's get out of here," she said as he set the tank back down, its gravel piled against one end and the stench of bottom sludge filling the room.

She slipped the net and bag into her purse and walked to the front door, cracking it open to check the street and sidewalk for anyone passing by. The man picked up his book and pamphlets, and they left as quickly as they had come.

* * *

Alex was waiting in the aquatics lab when Maria arrived. He hurried to meet her. "Maria, are you okay?"

"I'm fine, Alex. Why?"

"Nana called. She and Yolanda came home from shopping and found water all over the kitchen. I thought maybe you had trouble getting the stars to go in the bag."

"No, they're right here in my Tupperware bowl." Maria scowled. "Alex, I didn't make a mess in the kitchen. I was in the living room. Something doesn't sound right. Nana wouldn't call unless there was a problem. Would you mind going home to make sure everything's alright?"

"Not at all."

She gave him a quick hug and kiss. "I need to get the stars into the tank. Call me, please."

* * *

Janie sat in her "safe" chair in Jake's office—the one farthest from the trophies hanging on the wall. She checked her watch. Two minutes had passed since she last checked it. When would the waiting be over? Finally Jake's cell phone rang.

"Yeah?" he growled … . "You got them?" … "Meet me out front."

Jake turned to Janie. "The grandmother was gone," he told her. "No problems. I'm going to the parking lot to get the clones."

Janie let out a long sigh. "Thank God."

She had worried that Maria or her grandmother might have been home and be injured when Jake's team arrived. With the clones now in Jake's possession, she could relax—even start thinking about Doug getting his hand back. Jake's ethics might be questionable, but not his scientific skills. If the clones could induce human regeneration, he'd find out how.

It took Jake longer to return than she'd expected. When he finally came, he was livid.

"Fucking *guppies!*" he yelled, slamming the office door. "Nothing in the goddamn tank but guppies!" he repeated.

"They moved the clones?" Janie asked.

"Damn right they moved the clones, and I wonder why." His jaw worked as he stared at her. "You've been uptight about this all along."

Janie paled at the implication. "Daddy, I … okay, yes, I have. I admit it, but I still recognize that you have to get the clones to help Doug. I didn't warn her."

Jake looked away from her. "Had to be Belleville," he said, pressing his lips together. "They're at M-Gen now—under lock and key, and no way I can get them short of a major break-in."

Janie looked at him in alarm.

"No," he assured her. "Oh, I'd do it if I was sure they could induce human regeneration. But I'm not sure, and nobody can *be* sure without trials and test results, which I'm sure Belleville has started already." Jake extended his hand to touch Janie's. "Sorry, Baby. I wanted this maybe even more than you did. I'll continue to keep tabs on M-Gen, but meanwhile, I think Doug's only hope is for you to get chummy with your friend."

* * *

Maria grabbed the cell phone as soon as it rang. She'd been worried ever since Alex left.

"Alex! Is Nana okay?

"Yeah, she's fine—upset about the mess is all. We need to talk. You *do* have the stars, right?"

"Yes, they're right here. Alex what's going on?"

"I dunno. The aquarium's empty. Somebody dumped it in the kitchen sink and made a mess doing it. Looks to me like they were trying to steal the stars. That's why I asked if you had 'em."

"*Steal* the stars? Alex, who would try to steal them? Who except us knows they're even alive?"

"Only one name comes to mind. Janie must've seen them when she brought you home that day."

"Even so, why would she want to steal them? Besides me, only you and Dr. Belleville know of Veintidós' regenerative powers."

"Honey, she's Jake Blumenthal's daughter. I don't know who knows what or how, but I think we need to warn Belleville so he can beef up security around the lab. I'm coming back to M-Gen. Be thinking how we can convince Belleville to increase security without him learning about your three."

News of the attempted theft disturbed Maria so much, she completely forgot about the guppies. She'd gotten them a few months earlier for Nana to watch and seldom paid attention to them except to feed them and clean the tank—a busman's holiday.

HUMILITY

ONE WEEK LATER:

Maria looked up as Alex came through the double doors. She looked at her watch—past five o'clock. She'd been so busy teaching Veintidós new symbols, she'd completely lost track of the time.

"Hi, Honey," he said, turning down the aisle to the stars' tank. "I've got some good news and some other news, and I can already tell by the grin on your face that you're prob'ly gonna tell me that the stars are writing poetry or somethin', but let me go first, okay?"

"Okay." Maria laughed and kissed him hello. "What's your news?"

"Well, first, I succeeded in thawing out a couple of clones, so it looks like we'll have some more to put in the tank with your three. I slowed down the thawing rate, and that worked."

"I'm glad you found the problem," she said, then paused. "Do I want to know what the other news is?"

"Well, you're gonna hafta know since it involves you. Belleville's shutting down the aquatics lab."

"Shutting it *down*?" Maria cried. "But the stars … where will they—"

"It's okay, Honey," Alex hurried to assure her. "You and the stars stay; everything else goes."

None of the animals were being used in current research projects, and Belleville didn't want anyone else having an excuse to come into the lab. Just Maria, Alex, and him. He planned to have a guard post built outside the back door, and the door to the office wing would be keyed by a retinal scanner.

"*Santos*, Alex. He's really taking the stars' safety seriously."

"I don't know that it's the stars he's worried about so much as you."

"Me? Why is he worried about me?"

"Well, not exactly *you*. He's scared someone will be exposed to the rosemary smell. If you stay here in the lab, he can maintain a negative pressure in the room and keep the smell confined and out of the office areas. I honestly think he'd build an apartment here inside the lab for you, me, and Nana, if he thought we'd agree to stay in it."

"Alex, I'm being as careful as I can—avoiding contact with people. But I *have* to go out for school and shopping occasionally, and I can't tell Nana she has to stay in the house all day."

"I know, and Belleville understands, too. Nobody's criticizing you."

It was a risk they would have to deal with. Belleville had initiated some new tests with mice—to see if they would start regenerating if they were only exposed to the smell without Maria rubbing any of the substance on the wound. If they didn't regenerate, then that meant the agent wasn't transmitted by the smell.

"So … can I brag now? Is it my turn?" Maria asked.

"Yes, I'm ready to be astounded. What wonderful thing have they learned today?"

"To count," she said, beaming like a proud parent. "Not just displaying the numbers in sequence, but recognizing the significance of the symbols. They can tell how many items there are in a group and display the correct symbols. They even understand the concept of inequalities—'less than' and 'greater than.'"

Alex just shook his head. "Next you'll be tellin' me they can do math," he said.

"Actually, I already tried that," Maria admitted. "It's the strangest thing, Alex. They don't get it at all. They don't seem to have a clue what I'm trying to communicate when I show them how to add or subtract. Numbers, yes; arithmetic, no. Isn't that weird?"

"I dunno, Honey. To me, it's a relief. I was beginning to think they might be more intelligent than we are. I'm kinda glad you found something they *can't* do."

Maria pursed her lips. She didn't want to burst his bubble, but just because the stars couldn't do math didn't mean they were less intelligent than humans. Their intelligence might manifest in any number of other ways. They might be great logicians, artists, deep-thinking philosophers, who knew what else?

"Mankind has been humbled many times over the years. First we thought the Earth was the center of the universe, then the sun. Then we learned that our galaxy revolves around its own center and our sun is neither unique nor remarkable. Now, another demotion—we can't even brag that we're the only intelligent beings.

"Giving up that last claim of being special is going to be *very* difficult for a lot of people. It makes it all the more imperative that we free the stars and let them take charge of their own lives—seek their own destiny."

"Whew! Heavy stuff," Alex replied.

"Yes, it is, and it's a responsibility I'd like to have off of my shoulders as soon as we can make the arrangements. Dr. Belleville agreed to their release as one of the terms of our deal, and I'm going to hold him to his promise. His finger is regenerating, and that means the test is successful. We can release the stars now."

"When do you want to go?"

"I'm as ready as I'll ever be. My last final is day-after-tomorrow. We can go any time after that. Let's tell Dr. Belleville we want to go next week, if he can make the arrangements that soon."

"What are we gonna do about Nana? Will Yolanda be able to stay with her that long?"

"It will be asking a lot, but with Nana's mind improved so much, she may not require a lot of attention."

* * *

"I will go back to the care home," Nana declared, when Maria explained the situation.

"Nana, no," Maria cried. "There's no need for you to do that."

"Why not?" Nana asked. "They treated me well. The demen-tia ward wasn't bad. Now that you are my guardian, and I know I won't be stuck there, I'm fine staying there while you are away. It will give Yolanda a much needed break. Besides, my beloved sons pre-paid the first year. I would hate for them not to get their money's worth."

RELEASE

PUCALLPA, PERU:

The moto-taxi wended its way through the busy streets of downtown Pucallpa. The size of the town surprised Maria. She had expected a small fishing village with a population of a few hundred, not a few hundred thousand. In spite of its size, it was nothing like El Paso. The downtown area featured several restaurants and an open-air market, but many of the city's streets were unpaved. Outside of the core area, there were areas of severe poverty. Maria was thoroughly depressed by the time they reached their accommodations by the Ucayali River outside of town.

The appearance of their rental unit did nothing to improve her mood. It was one of three unpainted cabins strung out along a dirt path that angled toward the river. Someone had hacked the invading growth away from the buildings and the river side of the path, but head-high ferns and vines crowded the side opposite the river. Maria didn't see a single flower. The only positive quality she could find was the warm, humid, "green" smell that permeated the air. It reminded her of the aquatics lab and gave her hope that the stars would like their new home.

Maria hurried to help Alex get their luggage inside. It would be getting dark soon, and she didn't want to chance being bitten by mosquitoes. Inside, the rooms seemed small and the furnishings Spartan, but they were luxurious compared to some of the areas she had seen in town. At least it appeared clean.

She removed the stars' container from her backpack and placed it on a table. "I'm not looking forward to tomorrow," she said, sinking into a chair near the front window.

"I imagine not," Alex answered. "I've been wonderin' how you plan to release the stars. We'll be in a boat with a guide. He's likely to think it strange if you start talking to a bowl of water."

Maria shrugged. "Let him. I'm not going to just dump them and leave."

"Does it have to be where the original specimen came from? The river's a short walk from here. I'm sure the waters are all connected. You could release them in the little cove at the end of the path and have both time and privacy."

Maria looked out the window toward the river, its wide surface blotched with elongated shadows. "I'd like for them to know where their home is—I mean the place where the original *Pyramis nana* was found."

Suddenly Maria gasped. "Alex, someone's coming! Omigod! It's Janie. She must have found out … Alex, what'll we do?" Maria pulled the stars' container to her chest.

"We keep her away from the stars and get them to the river ASAP," he said.

There was no time for further development of the plan. Janie was walking up the path with a purposeful step. Maria's heart raced. She couldn't imagine how Janie had learned about the stars or what her intentions might be. Whatever they were couldn't be good.

"May I come in?" Janie asked as she reached the tiny porch.

Alex and Maria stood shoulder to shoulder blocking the door. "No," Alex said without hesitation. "You're not getting the stars."

"I don't want the stars."

Alex snorted. "Yeah, right. You're here. That means Geneering knows about the stars, and if Geneering knows about the stars, they want them."

"I'm not Geneering."

"Oh, come on! You think we're that naïve? The only way you could've learned about our plans is through your father. He must have bugs planted all over M-Gen."

"Please. I just want to talk."

"Is anyone else with you?" Maria asked, peering out into the gloom.

"Maria, no!" Alex yelled. "You can't trust her. She didn't fly three thousand miles just to talk."

"Janie, I have to agree with Alex. I'll give you a chance to talk, but you'll have to do things our way."

Janie nodded her agreement.

"Leave your purse on the steps," Maria instructed. "Raise your arms and turn around slowly."

Janie's face flushed red, but she complied with Maria's request.

Satisfied, Maria opened the screen door. "Sit there," she said, indicating the couch. "I'll listen to what you have to say, but you're not going to stop me from releasing the stars."

"Thank you." Janie said in a subdued voice. "I guess I can't blame you. But, I'm not going to try to talk you out of releasing the stars. I just want you to delay their release for a day or so, until I can get Doug to come."

"No way!" Alex yelled. "Doug's not getting anywhere near the stars."

"Alex, please, let her talk. Start from the beginning, Janie."

Maria had already surmised much of what Janie told them— that Doug had been frustrated, trying to lead the life his father chose for him instead of doing what he wanted to do, that he was basically a good person, once he got out from under his father's thumb. Janie had been helping him find himself when the accident occurred.

Janie looked at Maria. "I'm sorry. I'm the one who encouraged him to experiment with the stars. It's my fault he cut them, my fault he lost his hand." Her eyes shimmered with tears.

"He says he doesn't blame me, but our relationship has suffered. I'd begun losing hope of us getting married, then a miracle occurred, or it seemed like one to me. I was with Daddy at Geneering. He was playing the recordings from your office." She looked at Alex. "You were right about it being bugged. When I learned about Maria's arm growing and the stars' influence, I was ecstatic. It gave me hope Doug could get *his* hand back. Then I heard the next part—that M-Gen had destroyed the stars. The bottom dropped out from under me."

Maria nodded, remembering her own reaction to that news.

"Daddy got disgusted at that point," Janie continued. "He went out for a smoke and left the machine playing. When I learned you'd rescued the stars, I cried, I was so happy." She paused, shook her head, then looked at Maria. "I couldn't believe it when you said you wanted to release them. How could you do that? They were making your arm grow back. They could make Doug's hand grow back, or anybody else's."

The pain in Janie's voice was so intense, Maria felt her own tears well up. She joined her on the couch. She knew firsthand the emotional ordeal Janie had been through. She rested her hand on Janie's arm. Janie deserved to know why she was releasing the stars, but Maria would not allow her to talk her out of it. She was compassionate, but determined.

"Janie, you're my friend, and I will do everything I can to help you—to help Doug get his hand back, but you don't need the stars."

"That's not true, Maria. I heard you on the recording. You said the one called Veintidós was making your arm grow. How else would Doug get his hand back?"

"Veintidós did start my arm growing, but I can't share the process details with you. Alex is right. You may not be Geneering, but your father is. If I tell you, you'll tell him, and he'll try to beat M-gen getting the process to market. Or worse yet—and this is why I'm in such a hurry to free the stars—he might not even develop the process. If he got some of the stars, he could breed or clone them by the millions and make megabucks selling them to every hospital in the world. No one would ever have to lose an arm or a leg again."

"What would be so bad about that?"

"It sounds wonderful until you think about the details. What if all those millions of stars couldn't benefit their human captors unless they had one of their appendages cut off? When that one grew back they'd lose another one. Over and over again. What a horrible existence. I'd never be able to forgive myself if I were responsible for dooming them to that fate."

Maria turned to face Janie squarely. "Janie, the stars are not dumb animals. I've been communicating with them for weeks. They're intelligent beings—intelligent beyond anyone's imagination. We have no right to hold them in captivity and especially no right to maim them in order to exploit their regenerative capability for our own benefit. It's inhumane, inhuman, and immoral. You tell me what's the responsible, ethical, and moral thing to do."

Janie didn't answer. Maria studied her face and saw indecision and something else … guilt? Maria caught her breath. "Janie, is your father here?"

Janie hung her head and nodded.

"Alex," Maria yelled. "Help me get them to the river. Now!"

Maria darted across the room, grabbed the Tupperware bowl from the table, and bolted through the doorway, headed toward the river.

"Maria, wait! Come back!" Janie ran out the door after Maria with Alex close behind.

Maria ran down the path, shying away from its overgrown side. In the semi-darkness, every fern looked like fingers reaching for the stars. She held the container like a football, tucked in the crook of her left elbow, glancing back as she ran. Janie was less than a dozen feet behind her and Alex right on Janie's heels.

Maria pounded past the middle cabin, increasing the lead slightly. As she reached the path to the last cabin, a man burst from the darkness. Behind her Janie gasped.

"Daddy, no! Don't!"

Jake Blumenthal pulled a gun, aimed it at Maria, and shouted. "Hold it right there."

Maria heard the challenge and saw the gun, but had too much momentum to stop. She kept running, zig-zagging down the path.

"Goddammit, I said stop!" Jake took off after Maria, aiming a warning shot above her head. When he pulled the trigger, nothing happened. "What the hell?" he yelled, looking at the gun.

Maria heard the click behind her, then several more in succession. Jake, cursing in frustration, threw the gun at Maria, hitting her in the back of the head. She fell hard and the Tupperware bowl went rolling down the path.

Jake scooped it up like a football player grabbing a fumble. Alex lunged forward, caught Jake's trouser leg, and caused him to trip.

"Janie, catch," Jake yelled and tossed the bowl to Janie, who was now in the lead in the fateful game of leapfrog.

Janie caught the container. Her momentum carried her into the shallow water of the cove.

"Run!" Jake bellowed from his prone position.

Janie stared at the bowl in her hands.

Jake, no longer held by Alex, got up and lurched in Janie's direction. "Give it to me," he yelled.

He almost had his hands on the bowl, when Janie suddenly turned and hurled it into the water.

Maria watched in astonishment as the bowl sailed out over the water. It hit, went under, then bobbed to the surface. Maria's relief turned to panic when she realized the lid was still in place. The stars were trapped inside!

Jake waded into the river. Maria ran toward him, but knew he had too big a lead. He would get to the stars first.

"Piranhas!" she yelled. She had no idea if there were any in these waters, but hoped Jake was equally ignorant.

It worked. Jake stopped, turned, and clawed at the water to get out. It gave Maria all the advantage she needed. She dove headfirst into the river and reached the container in seconds. She jerked the lid off and upended it immediately, spilling the water and the stars into the river.

"Swim, Veintidós! All of you, swim," she cried. She watched them disappear, as tears streamed down her face.

Jake stood at the water's edge, looking bewildered. "You unloaded my gun? You helped her free them? Why, Janie? Why?"

"Because it was the right thing to do, Daddy. It was the right thing to do."

Jake glared at her, then turned and stomped off in the direction of their cabin with water squishing from his shoes at each step. "Your own goddamn father!" he ground out between clenched teeth.

Janie stood ankle-deep in the water. Her head drooped as her father walked away. Finally, she raised her eyes to meet Maria's.

"There's not much point in me saying I'm sorry. I made Daddy promise to let me try my way first—to get you to delay freeing the stars, so Doug could come. But I came prepared to help him try to steal them. Maria, I hope you can find it in your heart to forgive me."

Maria shrugged her shoulders. "I can't very well condemn you for doing the same thing I'd have done if our roles were reversed. Janie, I know, probably better than anyone, what Doug must be going through. I can't make promises, but I just ask that you be patient. Dr. Belleville is a compassionate person. I'm sure he will help Doug if he can."

Tears streamed down Janie's face as she embraced Maria. "Thank you," she whispered. She turned and followed her father.

SEPARATION

Maria's wet clothes dripped in the shower. The tiny sounds blended into the patter of light rain falling outside the cabin. She sat cross-legged on the bed, looking out the window.

"I didn't get to tell them goodbye," she said, sniffling and dabbing her red eyes.

Alex sat beside her and held her. "Maria, they're free, but they're not gone," he said.

"What's that supposed to mean?"

"It means they're still out there where you released them. Tomorrow morning we can go back to the cove. I'll bet if you call them, they'll come."

"Oh, Alex, do you think so?" Maria's face showed a glimmer of hope.

"Yes, I do. Considering all that's happened to them, they've gotta be scared to death. I think they'll huddle together and stay in that little cove until they have a chance to explore their surroundings. They should be near enough to hear you when you call."

Maria kissed him and laid her head against his chest, exhausted. Alex eased her back on the bed and pulled her close. She snuggled against him, relaxing for the first time in … she couldn't think when.

* * *

Gray clouds hung low in the morning sky, but Maria was grateful the rain had stopped. It would be impossible to see the stars with rain dimpling the water's surface. She stood thigh-deep in the tannin-stained water, looking across the cove to the wide, slow river beyond. She had called the stars several times, but only saw an occasional turtle, snake, or ripple from a fish's dorsal fin.

The jungle hushed briefly each time she called, then returned to its raucous babble.

Alex waited on the bank. "Louder," he encouraged.

"Queridos!" Maria managed a bit more volume—the best she could do with the lump in her throat. She was beginning to despair. Once more she called, but her voice broke. "They're not coming."

Her shoulders sagged as she turned toward Alex and slogged toward the bank.

"Look!" Alex pointed.

She spun around to see a tiny wake on the surface—something moving toward her, half in and half on the water, like a fishing lure being slowly reeled in.

Maria's legs churned to propel her through the water, but she ended up tripping herself and fell to her knees. She reached out to the star that swam toward her. The water was too dark to tell which one. A thrill washed over her as three appendages and a shorter fourth wrapped around her finger, squeezing gently.

"Veintidós! Oh, Veintidós," she cried. "Where are the others?" Tears blinded her. She couldn't have seen them even if they were there.

Veintidós loosened her grip on Maria's finger, but remained close to her hand. "#1 AND #13 NOT COME," she signaled.

"They're not coming? But why? I mean ... Veintidós teach Maria."

"#1 AND #13 TASTE FREE."

Maria frowned, trying to make sense of the words. "You mean they're exploring? What about you? You came back. Veintidós taste free?"

"#22 TASTE FREE. #22 TASTE MANY WORD WITH MARIA. FREE LESS THAN WORD WITH MARIA. #22 WITH MARIA AND ALEX GO."

Maria clutched her chest. "*Ay, me rompe el corazón.*" She whispered. Her eyes filled with tears again.

* * *

"Why the long face?" Alex asked once they were comfortable back at the cabin. "Veintidós chose to stay with you, and the other stars are free—the ones that want to be anyway. I'd think you'd be happy."

"I should be … I *am* happy that Veintidós is coming back with us, but it's a major complication. Much as I hated to release the stars, at least doing so would have freed me of the responsibility for their safety and welfare. Now I'm too worried to be happy. Janie and her father don't know I can trigger regeneration. They think Veintidós is causing my arm to regenerate, and she is, or *was*. What if they find out we're bringing her home with us? Janie might not make the same decision next time, and we already know what her father will do and would likely do if he knew about me."

"We'll need to alert Belleville before we head home so he can tighten security. But you're gonna hafta explain why you're bringing one back."

"Oh, you're right." She grimaced. "I don't know if I'm ready to do that yet."

"Well, before we do *anything*, we'd better make sure Janie and her father are gone. With Veintidós out of the water, she's vulnerable again. Let's go up to the rental office and ask some questions. Do you think you can coax Veintidós into a water bottle?"

"I hope so. Dr. Belleville didn't arrange permits for us to bring specimens *back*. We're going to have to sneak her through security at the airport."

* * *

A dark skinned child with jet-black hair peeked out from behind the rental agent's leg, sucking on her thumb. She stared, wide-eyed at Maria's stunted arm, forgetting the thumb in her mouth. Maria smiled at her and the girl moved further behind the man until only one eye remained visible. The man told Maria that Janie and Jake had checked out earlier.

"Ask him if we can move into their cabin," Alex suggested. "It's closer to the water."

The man shook his head when she asked. "Some men already rented it," she translated.

"Rats. Okay, we'll manage where we are. What do you want to do?"

"Alex, I need a break. Can we just go into town and see whatever there is to see?"

They found brochures in the rental office. The agent told Maria the Parque Natural was a zoo. They decided to go there, do some shopping, and have an early dinner. Restaurant Anaconda, according to the brochure, was 'considered by some to be the best seafood restaurant in the Amazonas.' That appealed to Alex.

"It sounds nice," Maria agreed. "I'll ask the man to call us a mototaxi. Let's go back to the cabin and change while we're waiting."

* * *

NEXT MORNING:

"Alex, I'm going to take Veintidós to the cove and release her to see if she can find Trece and Número Uno. I still want to tell them goodbye."

"You want me to come with you?"

"No, I'm just going to put her in the water. I'll only be a minute."

Maria slung her backpack over one shoulder and headed for the river. The last time she was on that path, she was in a panic to release the stars. Now she was trying to get them back—at least long enough to give them a proper goodbye.

The door of the last cabin opened as Maria passed by. She was glad Janie and Jake were gone. She could very easily have had a repeat encounter with Jake Blumenthal—this time without Alex's help. She quickened her pace, watching as a brawny, sunburned man in Bermuda shorts stepped out and down the steps, carrying a box and towing a piece of luggage. Maria exhaled with relief when he turned toward the rental office. She knelt in the shallow water and popped the lid from the Tupperware bowl.

"Veintidós, find Número Uno and Trece. Dark, light. Maria come."

"Hey! Señorita. Get out of there!"

Maria had barely upended the bowl when the sunburned man grabbed her arm. He pulled her to her feet and dragged her back several steps. She swung her backpack at him, but the makeshift weapon contained nothing heavy or hard. Surprisingly, he let go. She crouched, ready to attack.

"Easy, lady. I'm not going to hurt you. I just had to get you out of the water." He held up his hands and backed away from her. "Sorry if I scared you. You speak English?"

Maria straightened from her crouch, nodded, but remained wary.

"Look," the man said, "I'm a biologist. There's a whole team of us here looking for a new species of animal that's supposed to be in these waters. One of my buddies got bitten. They were supposed to put up warning signs, but nobody's done it yet."

"Bitten?" Maria didn't trust her voice to ask more.

"Yeah. We captured a couple of specimens and one of them bit him."

"*Dios*, no!"

"Don't worry. He'll be all right. We came prepared for it. Listen, I gotta go. Our plane leaves in a couple of hours. Sorry about manhandling you."

* * *

Maria sprinted up the path to the cabin, screaming Alex's name. He burst through the doorway, meeting her a few feet from the cabin.

"Maria! What happened? Are you okay?"

"They've got the stars," she said, her breath coming in gasps.

"Who has the stars?"

"Geneering."

"How can they have the stars?"

"The man told me."

"What man? No. Wait. Start from the beginning. Tell me what happened. Slowly."

Maria was too upset to talk slowly. She let it all out in a rush—about the man in the last cabin following her, pulling her from the water just as she released Veintidós … saying it was dangerous to go in the water … telling her they captured two stars and one of them bit his coworker.

"How do you know they're from Geneering?" Alex asked.

"Because Jake Blumenthal is the only one who knows where the stars are and has the resources to get a team here this soon. Oh, Alex, they've got Número Uno and Trece!" she wailed.

"Honey, we don't know that. We put more'n two dozen stars in the river. There's no reason to assume they got either of your favorites."

"Oh, Alex. What are we going to do?"

"Well, right now there's not much we *can* do—not until Veintidós returns."

Alex slid his arms around her, but suddenly she pushed away from him. "Alex, we have to tell Dr. Belleville! Janie and her dad heard me say Veintidós was making my arm grow. With the stars they captured, Geneering will be able to duplicate the discovery and maybe even beat Dr. Belleville exploiting it."

COMPETITION

It seemed to Alex the phone rang forever. It was Sunday morning. Maybe Belleville had gone to church. Finally a raspy voice answered.

"Dr. Belleville? It's Alex Goodson."

"Goodson, do you have any idea what time it is?"

Alex didn't. He'd completely forgotten that Pucallpa was two time zones east of El Paso. "I, ah … I'm sorry, sir. We have a problem."

"Very well, let's hear it," he growled.

Alex explained about the bugs at M-Gen, how Jake Blumenthal and Janie had learned about Maria's arm and the stars, and had followed them to Peru.

"They tried to steal the stars from us before we could release them," Alex told him.

"Good God!" Belleville shouted, fully awake now. "How did…? You say *tried*? Does that mean they were unsuccessful?"

"Yes and no. They got the container away from us, but Janie must've changed her mind at the last second. She threw it into the river."

"Then they *didn't* get them. Good! Geneering learning about the discovery is terrible news, but without any stars to work with the knowledge will be of little use to them."

"That's just it, sir. They *did* get some stars. Maria was so upset after their release, I took her to town for the day, so she could wind down. When we got back we found out a bunch of men from Geneering went into the little cove where we released the stars and captured two of them. One of the men got bitten."

Belleville took so long to respond, Alex began to worry that the connection had been broken, or worse yet, that Belleville had suffered a heart attack.

"Goodson, if Geneering learns the secret to human regeneration, I could be destroyed financially—M-Gen as well."

"I understand, sir, but there may still be some good news."

"I'll take anything you offer," Belleville answered in a subdued voice.

"If I remember right, you said the other star that Doug cut—the one you took home—didn't give off the rosemary smell."

Belleville confirmed Alex's memory was correct. Alex's theory was that the ordinary stars might not produce the substance that triggers regeneration. Perhaps only the three special stars exhibited that capability. In fact, it could be only one of them—Veintidós.

"We know that one was not captured," Alex told him.

"*Not* captured, you say? How would you know that?"

"Because Maria nearly freaked out at the possibility that Geneering might have taken her favorite star. She went down to the river and called it, and it came."

That wasn't exactly the truth, but close enough.

"She *called* it? Bloody effing hell, man! Get her down there and have her call it again. Call *all* of them. Find out which ones Geneering got and notify me immediately. This information is crucial, Goodson—*crucial*, do you hear me?"

"Yes, sir. I'll get back to you as soon as we know."

* * *

The following morning, Alex accompanied Maria to the muddy riverbank. The day was gray, reflecting both of their moods. A crooked post with a freshly-painted sign stood several feet out in the water—PELIGRO—danger, in bold red letters. Maria kicked off her sandals, but Alex stopped her from stepping into the water.

"We both know it's safe," he said, "but we don't want to attract attention."

He listened while Maria called out to the stars. He knew *queridos* was a Spanish term of endearment, but she also called each star by name—also in Spanish. Maybe he should take some classes. It would please Maria. Her grandmother, too. He needed to start thinking about the three of them instead of just himself.

Silence interrupted his train of thoughts. Maria had stopped calling. Her shoulders sagged like she'd lost her best friend. Not an inappropriate analogy, he realized. Keeping her spirits up the next few days would be a challenge.

He slid his arm around her waist. "Honey, the cove looks small to us, but I'm sure it seems huge to the stars. It may take Veintidós a while to find them. We'll come back at noon and again before sundown."

Alex picked up the backpack and took Maria's hand for the walk back to the cabin.

The next day was a repeat of the first day. Likewise the third and the fourth, with Maria becoming more depressed after each failure. By the fifth day, Alex was ready to concede that Maria was right—Geneering had captured the two intelligent stars and would undoubtedly do exactly as she feared—amputate their appendages.

Now they faced a new problem. They couldn't call off the search until Veintidós returned. Also, they couldn't go home for the same reason. Alex knew Maria wouldn't leave without Veintidós. As they approached the river, he tried to think how to broach the subject with her, but a scream interrupted his thoughts.

"Veintidós!" Maria fell to her knees in the shallow water and scooped up the star in her hands. "Oh, Alex, look at her! She's so thin!"

Alex tried to get Maria to bring Veintidós back to the cabin where they wouldn't attract so much attention. She could give her something to eat there, but Maria shook her head.

"We have to wait for the others," she said, filling the Tupperware bowl with river water. She let Veintidós slide from her hands.

"Maybe she didn't find them," Alex replied.

Maria peered down into the tannin-stained water. "Veintidós, Número Uno and Trece come?"

"NOT COME," the star replied.

Maria sank to the ground. Alex grabbed the container with one hand while trying to support her with the other. He knelt beside her. "It doesn't mean Geneering got them," he said. "Come on, Honey. Let's get her back to the cabin."

ETHOS

Veintidós floated in a clear drinking glass in the middle of the small kitchen table, grabbing at flakes of fish food. The rounded surface magnified her body, making it easy to see her dappled skin and her beige borders. Maria and Alex crowded together on one side of the table to find out what had happened to the other stars.

"#22 FIND #1 AND #13," Veintidós displayed.

"*Oh, gracias a Dios*," Maria cried out, clutching Alex's arm. She tried to hold back the tears so she could see the patterns, but had to wipe her eyes before the next one formed.

"#1 AND #13 WITH OTHER STARS. #13 PUSH OTHER STARS."

"Push?" Alex asked. "I don't get it."

"I think she means Trece has taken control of the other stars," Maria answered. "Push would make sense. She always bossed them at M-Gen."

Veintidós began flashing patterns again. Maria cut her commentary short.

"MANY HAND WITH NET COME. #13 FEAR HAND WITH NET. #13 TEACH OTHER STARS BITE HAND WITH NET. #13 BITE HAND. OTHER STARS BITE HAND."

"No! She mustn't teach them that."

"#1 BITE #13. #13 BITE #1. OTHER STARS BITE #1. #1 LESS THAN #1."

"Alex, he's hurt!"

Maria lowered her face even with the glass. "Veintidós, can you show us … I mean … ." She forced herself to think with the limited vocabulary they had developed. "Veintidós find Número Uno. Maria go with Veintidós. Número Uno and Veintidós come with Maria. Maria feed Número Uno. Número Uno more than Número Uno."

"What good will feeding him do?" Alex asked.

"I don't know how to say 'nurse back to health'. That was as close as I could come. If she can find him maybe I can help him. I *have* to. He tried to stop Trece from hurting the men."

Veintidós displayed a dark, undulating pattern Maria had never seen before. A feeling of dread crept over her.

"DARK LIGHT. #1 EQUAL ZERO."

"No! Alex, no."

Maria pressed her forehead against his chest, keening softly. She hadn't expected the stars to live long after their release, but she never counted on being there and learning how or when one of them died.

"Please, Alex, I want to go home."

Alex held her for a moment, then released her. "Yeah. Even with Veintidós' help we'd never find and capture Trece. She's got the ordinary stars to live with. She's better off living free."

Maria inhaled a long, ragged breath, then lowered her face to the star's level. "Maria and Alex and Veintidós go home."

She started to pick up the glass and return Veintidós to her plastic container, but saw patterns forming.

"#22 NOT GO. #22 WITH #1. DARK LIGHT #1 EQUAL ZERO."

Maria started to cry again—this time for a different reason. She'd seen Número Uno and Trece rally around Veintidós when Doug cut her, but didn't realize or recognize that the stars felt compassion for one another. The discovery filled her with an incredible feeling of awe. She located a blank flash card and sketched a heart with a red marker, printing LOVE beneath it.

"Veintidós *love* Número Uno," she enunciated, holding up the symbol and new vocabulary word.

"#22 ♥ #1," the star answered, using the symbol instead of the word. "#22 ♥ MARIA. #22 ♥ #13." Then Veintidós reproduced the dark, undulating pattern she had displayed earlier—the one Maria sensed meant 'sorrow'. "MARIA AND ALEX GO. #22 WITH #1. #22 WITH #13. LIGHT DARK NO COUNT. #22 TEACH #13 ♥ HAND."

Maria couldn't stop the tears. She didn't even try. Alex came behind her and wrapped his arms around her while she wept.

"Y' know," he said, "I worried what was going to happen when we released an intelligent species into the wild. I'm not worried any more. Veintidós could teach us humans a thing or two about ethos."

EPILOGUE

"Mama, why can't Daddy ride with us?"

Maria looked in the rear-view mirror. Kinky red curls stuck out above Emma's car seat.

"Because Daddy is driving Miss Janie's car."

"Why?"

"He is bringing the car so Miss Janie and Mr. Doug can drive it home when they get off the ship."

"Why did Miss Janie go on the ship?"

Maria smiled. The *why*'s would keep coming until something new caught Emma's attention. Then they would begin again.

"To be with Mr. Doug," she answered. "Look, Emma. I see it coming."

Maria watched the cruise ship move majestically up the channel, dazzling white in the midday sun. "Keep your buckle snapped until we park. We have plenty of time before people begin to disembark."

"What is *distant bark*, Mama?"

"Dis-*em*-bark, Emma. *Barco* means ship. *Disembark* means get off the ship."

"Why do they call it *Barco Milagro*?"

"Because it's a hospital ship where wonderful things happen. Some people call them miracles."

"Why?"

Maria arched her back as the baby pushed its foot into her kidney. Soon there would be two to ask questions.

"Here comes Daddy," she said to divert Emma's attention. "Ask him if he'll put you on his shoulders so you can look for Nana."

"Is Nana going back on the ship?"

"Yes, Querida."

"But why? I want her to come home with us."

"Nana works on the ship to help people. She'll stay with us after we get back from Pucallpa."

"Pucallpa? We're going to Pucallpa? When? Can I swim naked? Will Veintidós be there? Are you going to cry again if Trece comes? Daddy, Daddy! We're going to Pucallpa!"

Alex grabbed Emma, tossed her in the air, then caught her and settled her on his shoulders. He stooped to kiss Maria.

"How you doing, Honey?"

Maria put her arm around him and matched steps as they walked. "I'm your wife, I'm pregnant with your child, and I'm happier than I've ever been in my life."

After retiring from a thirty-year career in aerospace, then working another ten in communication, Paul A. Bussard is finally free to devote his time to writing. Mostly he likes to write hard science fiction, but he's also a published poet. He earned a B.S. degree in Mathematics from Wichita State University and has a heavy background in the physical sciences. Mr. Bussard lives near Houston, Texas where he is an active member of the Woodlands Writers' Guild.